We dedicate this book to our fathers. They are no longer with us, but their inspiration lives on. Thank you both.

To the Führer he had been "the Toymaker".
To his original lord, centuries ago – "the Clockmaker".
Necromancy within both.
Now there.
There was the truth within.

THE CLOCKMAKER

*"No man in this world may boast of his might,
he is awake in the morning and dead at night."*

THE
CLOCKMAKER

DREW NEARY AND
CERI WILLIAMS

Matador
9 Priory Business Park,
Wistow Road, Kibworth Beauchamp,
Leicestershire. LE8 0RX
Tel: 0116 279 2299
Email: books@troubador.co.uk
Web: www.troubador.co.uk/matador
Twitter: @matadorbooks

ISBN 978 1788034 586

British Library Cataloguing in Publication Data.
A catalogue record for this book is available from the British Library.

Printed and bound by CPI Group (UK) Ltd, Croydon, CR0 4YY
Typeset in 11pt Minion Pro by Troubador Publishing Ltd, Leicester, UK

Matador is an imprint of Troubador Publishing Ltd

CERI WILLIAMS
Author

Ceri Williams was born in Chester, lived in several countries before settling in the East Midlands.

Graduating from the University of the Witwatersrand with a degree in Dramatic Arts and English, she then worked in advertising as a copywriter before moving to the UK and becoming a teacher.

She has always loved language, be it the spoken, the written or the performed, and has been writing in one form or another, since the beginning of time!

The Clockmaker marks the start of a long term collaboration of two authors- Drew Neary and Ceri Williams and the artist Ana Priscila Rodriguez Aranda.

DREW NEARY

Author

Andrew grew up in North East of England where as a teenager he nurtured a deep fascination with science, science fiction, fantasy and mythology and rock music.

Since graduating from University in Leicester he developed a passion for writing. He has turned his hand to many a profession – from driving tractors to teaching science in higher education but the wish to write always remained.

He wrote several short stories, and after meeting Ceri, began to co-write the novel Optics from which The Clockmaker was born.

Andrew lives in Leicestershire with his young family. In his spare time he enjoys tabletop wargames, online gaming and walking football.

ANA PRISCILA
RODRIGUEZ ARANDA

Visual artist

Priscila Rodriguez was born in Mexico City, 1974 and now resides in The Netherlands since 1998.

She graduated from the Academy of Fine Arts in Utrecht in 2006 specialising in Inter-media and Photography; she has also studied History and Graphic Design.

She currently works in developing her own photographic techniques, combining digital and three dimensional elements.

She started working with the classical forms of drawing and painting until she discovered the magic of antique photographs and old papers left behind in flea markets; which she has been obsessively collecting for more than a decade. The fascination for the old and the forgotten are the key elements for her work and the stories she tells.

In addition to exhibitions in Mexico and The Netherlands, she has also collaborated in publications. The Clockmaker is her first book cover.

The atmosphere of the novel and the nature of her "time based" visuals makes the ongoing collaboration of Ana Priscila Rodriguez Aranda and Drew Neary and Ceri Williams the perfect triage.

For more of her work, visit: www.priscila.nl and http://www.allthingslostonearth.com/

I

Memories

Memories. Berlin. Pockets of time fading away within his ancient mind like wisps of smoke in the air. The leavings of the engine's smoke stack pulling this carriage northwards, as he watched them drift past the window and unravel. Ah, those thoughts would fade so easily.

Berlin would always surface. No matter where he had been since. Sleeping, waking, walking foreign streets. Berlin would rise above his other horrors that stretched away like failed crusades. Centuries littered with lives.

No matter how deftly he tried to bury her, she clawed through the meat of his mind with broken nails. Accusing him with cold Soviet eyes – and he would remember. Flitting across his eyelids in an endless loop. Remember. The eyes of the guards. The sounds of the troops. The feel of the chains. The odours in the fires.

II

Meetings

Dimly the voices of a mother and a child penetrated these thoughts. Whispering, chiding, excited as the small boy glimpsed marvels through the window of the train, wiping moisture away from the glass to peer closely at sheep, pheasants that fluttered in fright at the steam engines passing. Their human presence snuffed the images away and he felt a moment of gratitude for the company of voices. A normality within a crowded train of lives en route to elsewhere.

He leant back against the padded headrest, a wry smile forming as he allowed his hand to slide back into the pocket of his greatcoat. Despite it being a summer's day he still felt the cold. Still felt the need for the weight and warmth of this garment.

Such a glorious piece of magic within. His fingers began to caress the abdomen, brushing against intricate brass cogs that started to click with glacial grace at his touch. Barely moving his fingers, he checked each joint, bone and wire, knowing so intimately where each was placed, their roles and relationships in this construct's purpose. Tooth enamel, roots removed, arranged as armour plates, polished, perfect for their intended task. Like a clock they ticked. Winding their metallic cogs through the other, oiled, primed.

He slipped his fingertips across the smooth carapace once more, like one may a favoured lap-pet, as the greenery of Northumberland passed endlessly and his thoughts turned to his soul's freedom; waiting, finally, at the very end of this line.

III

Then

During the autumn and winter that first year they would wake each morning, pleased to have survived the night, and simply got on with their day.

So many of their friends had been evacuated. But for Annette, this was her home. It was Gordon's. And she would be here waiting for him on his return. The Fosters had urged her to travel to them, and for a while as the schools closed and the city she loved became wracked and torn, she was tempted. But in the end, a stubbornness she hadn't known she possessed took hold of her and she stayed.

Rationing was beginning to bite and they had started a market garden. She eventually allowed Duncan to venture out in the mornings, to check on the chickens and water the vegetables. The garden was often covered in little strips of shrapnel and leaflets in German. In time they must have become immune to noise, with the raids starting as soon as it was dark, and lasting till daylight.

*

Annette eased into a mother's proud smile as she watched her son's adventure along the corridor. The carriage unsteadily crossed the joints between the rails but Duncan paid it little heed, arms spread wide as he raced along; a Spitfire today, tomorrow a Lancaster.

The noises peaked as further up the carriages, another lad spread his wings too, and machine gun clatter echoed throughout the corridors. She hadn't noticed the moment the other child had eased into the game of war, and suddenly panicked that she had let her guard lapse. Duncan had never left her sight for a moment. Not for years now. Natural, they said; her friends had been reassuring, almost pious, after her loss, "after what you have been through". But she knew it was tinged through with something else. Call it a feeling if you will, or a mother's intuition, but it was there. Rooted in her. A terror so deep she dare not give it a voice or form, until it sprang from her at times like this. Times when she had relaxed just enough to hear things outside of herself.

With a final rattle of artillery fire, Duncan's newfound friend spread-eagled himself in mock defeat near the exit to the baggage hold. Applause rippled from compartments and couples standing by the open windows in the corridors – admiration for the boys' dramatic conclusion to their dogfight. Britain's skies were once more cleared of the threats of the evil Luftwaffe. The battle once more played out by the innocent… *"so much owed by so many to so few"*. Proudly she listened to the comments of fellow travellers: "Lovely lad", "good-looking boy". He was. He definitely was. Stronger now they had left the city. Bags of boiled sweets and toffees were produced and shared. Such small moments of joy were a welcome respite from the months of the Blitz.

Ah Gordon, if only you could see him right now. He is so happy. Found a friend. They are running and playing as though all that we left behind has never occurred. No long nights without you.

"That was such good fun," he said breathlessly, nudging her back to the present. She smiled and held him tightly and said that he was by far the best pilot in the Royal Air Force. "Your father would be so proud of you, my love."

Duncan settled next to her, offering her a toffee, pocketing the rest. She thought the game would have tired him out but soon he began to squirm restlessly on the seat, asking where they were and when they would be arriving. There was no sign of the ticket collector or porters. Duncan's attention strayed from his mother towards the elderly man seated next to the window. Annette had been aware of him, his stillness. His winter greatcoat firmly buttoned, despite the balm of the day and the stuffiness of the carriage, whose windows were sealed shut with grime and rust. Old and deeply tanned, lined like the fallen leaves in Jesmond Park. He had been the only one who had ignored the boisterous boys.

When she had got up earlier to check on her child, the man had caught her glance, and instead of returning her smile had abruptly turned to stare at the landscape beyond the windows. Into that border world becoming steadily steeper, with stern hills whose greyness uprooted the forests and woods. She had thought it rude and untoward, and for a moment felt embarrassed.

Duncan turned abruptly to the man next to the window who had ignored them both. Annette began to pull him gently back suggesting they find the guard to ask about the time they were meant to arrive.

"Would you like a sweet?" he asked. "I've got quite a lot from the other people."

Annette shushed him and told him that he shouldn't bother any more people. They were nearly there and to be a bit more patient. Besides, the gentleman might be deaf and not want to talk. Surprisingly she heard him reply. He spoke with an accent, softly thanking her son. He would be delighted to have a sweet.

Duncan produced a selection and held them over the seat.

"The toffee's nice and there's a butterscotch one too. You suck them for ages and they still taste lovely."

"Thank you," the old man replied. "Would you like some chocolate?" Annette was unsure of her role within this. Should she be polite and introduce them both? Or let her child talk to the man on his own? Either way she would appear rude. Almost as rude as his earlier snub. But his accent confirmed he was a stranger here, and English etiquette may be foreign in his country. So many people left rudderless by the war years.

Satisfied she had sorted that out in her own mind, she stood up and offered her hand. The old man took it, limply holding hers before letting his drop back into his pocket. His expression didn't alter. It was a cursory, brief exchange between strangers. An interlude between small northern stations.

Duncan crouched over the seat, blissfully unaware of her tension, focused on the moment with the fascination of children for oddities.

"Chocolate? Have you got chocolate? Americans have chocolate. Are you American?" The old man's gaze flicked briefly towards Annette and something furtive appeared within the glance, leaving her with an aftertaste of unease.

It was such a terribly minute moment though, so fleeting, yet one that would later return to her in a moment of terrible fear.

"American? Mmm. Can you keep a secret, little one?" The old man raised a finger to his lips. "Shall we ask your mother?" as inch-by-inch, the foil wrapping of a chocolate bar edged out of his pocket. A rectangular brown wrapper. With a word in bold. A veritable lure for this perfect, perfect child.

Annette thanked the man. Of course, she said, but only a small bit, her son had already had far too much sugar for one day. She rose and gave their excuses, explaining that she needed to enquire how much longer it would be until they reached Lochnagar.

"We have a hotel," added Duncan, chocolate clutched in a happy hand.

"He was a nice man, wasn't he Mummy? That old man." Distracted, Annette nodded, searching through her bag for the tickets for the collector. Why on earth did she purchase such a ridiculously large handbag? It was impossible to find anything even when she wasn't feeling rushed.

"That chocolate was delicious – he said there was more where that came from when he sees me again too."

As the mother and child walked away, the old man bowed his head, slipping the Hershey bar back into his coat. As he did so, an oddly pitched sound rose from within the pocket. A feral sound of claws and clicks. The old man for one moment looked startled before running his tongue along his stolen teeth and smiled.

And now it begins.

IV

Life

Life in London during the Blitz had gone on very much as usual for Annette and Duncan. School, homework, friends for tea. Sometimes they would go to the theatre during the morning as a treat, but be home before the sirens. Travelling in on the Tube they would peep through the netted windows that had a little spy hole in the middle, to work out where the worst raids had occurred the previous night. The rescue squads would be clearing up; tiles on the roofs would be standing to attention, curtains stripped by flying glass, doors and windows missing, and sometimes just piles of new rubble. But of course, that wasn't the worst of it. The deaths. Bless them. Firemen would be damping down the fires, and the wardens clearing a street of people waiting for the army bomb disposal team.

Duncan liked their uniforms. Mummy said they looked very smart. They wore black battle dress and trousers and a steel helmet painted black with the letters ARP in white on the front. They all carried a police whistle and a torch, a haversack that held a first aid kit, and their own gas mask. Duncan thought they were very brave because they didn't sleep at night, but made sure everyone was safe and all the lights were out.

He wondered if he might get a torch for Christmas.

*

The porter lowered the leather suitcases from the carriage. There was leftover rain on the platform and she grasped her child's hand tightly so he didn't slip. They made their way into the single storey wooden station building, yellow boards freshly painted, some bedding plants in bloom. She enquired at the kiosk if it were far to Lochnagar. Apparently it wasn't, replied the stationmaster, two miles or so, but too far to walk, especially with a bairn. Could he ring the village for a horse and trap? One would collect them within the hour then.

Her boy bounced excitedly on the seat as they passed by mists and mountains, asking so many questions of the driver that Annette's head began to ache. Rain began to sluice across the flat highlands of deer and bracken and the driver stopped to raise the cover.

Despite the beauty of their new landscape, anxiety crept upon her again. Could she make this work? Would she manage to be both father and mother? Would he be lonely in this isolated house – before he started school and made friends? Gordon had spent his childhood years here, speaking of the house and the village with such affection, so many memories, places he wanted to show his child. Burns, lochs, waterfalls. They had planned to spend each summer here after the war.

Before her thoughts could tip into grief, the driver said they were practically there.

Dropping them off next to a lynch gate, the sound of the hooves drew away from them into the dusk, towards where a signpost pointed to Lochnagar.

Pillars topped by fauns, their sandstone features smeared and eroded, sat on either side of the long driveway that stretched straight and pebbled to the house. Surrounded by land and loch, a backdrop of mountains slotted into their earth sockets, range upon range.

Like teeth.

The gate was firmly chained with a heavy-cast heart padlock. Somewhere on the set of keys she had received from the solicitor would be a small one to slip beneath the cover. Annoyed by her cumbersome choice of bag yet again, she finally located them in an inner pocket. Duncan excitedly unlocked the gate, leaving her to gaze beyond him at the house, sprawling across a neglected lawn. Overgrown and spiked with dandelion heads, small intruder breezes sent several scurrying away and she wondered how long it would take her to mow it.

They had only seen pictures of this house. An old

hunting lodge. Her heart sank as they got closer and she could see that years of harsh winters had battered a once sturdy facade. Ivy had crept unheeded, digging tendrils into steel grey bricks. Spreading across the three-storey house unrepentantly. It completely covered one of the large bay windows in the left portion of the lodge. She dreaded to think what the state of the inside was like, after all these years of it being empty.

It seemed to be all angles and jutting roofs. She had no idea how many chimneys there were. Twin fronts were separated by a narrower part of the house. Each with three windows, one above the other. Duncan counted nine. *Oh dear*, she thought, *so many windows to clean.* Curtains were drawn tightly across them and gave the house a hopeless look. Across the full length of the house ran a verandah, sagging slightly, and as they drew closer she could see the rust on the filigree posts.

Apart from the green riot of ivy, there was an overwhelming feel of greyness. Grey chimneys, grey slate, grey brick, grey stairs mounting to the front door.

For a fleeting moment she doubted the wisdom of moving them here. But what choice really had she had? After their small home had been destroyed, it was the suggestion of the Fosters they go and move nearby. It would have meant selling this childhood home of Gordon's though, and she had lost so much of him already. Newcastle wasn't too far by train and she hoped that Walter and Nora would come and stay with them when she had tackled the most urgent repairs. They had said they would, of course.

Duncan pointed to one of three dormer windows, sharp roofs and the remains of roof crenellations. "I'd like to sleep up there in the attics, Mummy. It will be fun!"

Bless her child; he managed to bring joy to the grimmest of moments.

This door key was bulky and heavy, but at least she found it with ease on the key chain. Yes, Duncan could be the first to open the door to their new home. It was much, much larger than their old home, he said, and she agreed. It was almost intimidating.

What would they find within? Thin dust and sadness?

V

Perfection

Stopping frequently on this long journey, he had used the time to stretch his legs along station platforms and look at his surroundings, the small construct within his pocket silent and still on these occasions. He would touch it from time to time. For comfort and admiration.

It was strange, he reflected, how after six years of sinister glory, he was now a forgotten part of the fallen Reich. Hiding now beneath this greatcoat and borrowed accent, moving between packing crates and the scattered suitcases of people who, like him, were travellers.

Oddly, there were no guards on these trains, nor was this journey's destination to places of unspeakable horror.

He had seen men in uniform though, khaki, twill and navy, caps and berets. Some with families, some in groups. Smoking, leaning against the sides of the buildings, canvas sacks discarded at their feet. They comfortably mingled with passengers boarding or leaving through station buildings whose wrought-iron canopies were rusting. Red brick and grey. Names he couldn't pronounce. Accents he found difficult to discern. And always the mountains doused in mist.

Clouds would lift and occasional patches of leaden sky would be alive with birds that dipped and wheeled on vast wings around the steam from the engine. Copses of trees on rocky outcrops, their endless sheep grazing. But he never saw homes. Never.

So odd.

In his recent homeland, with its beauty and colour, there were the framed houses; churches whose spires over-towered long valleys where the salmon leapt. But here, apart from the endless stations, there were no lights from farms or towns. He was used to summits. The loftiness of the Alps, crags towering above valleys where water flowed and the scent of summer lingered. These hills and ranges edging the landscape possessed a mysticism he found alluring. Peering at him through this carriage window, where the pasts of other travellers lingered in the tartan fabric of the seats.

They had turned west for some hours now, heading towards the sea and open spaces. He gazed out as they passed furrowed fields of things yet to grow. Towards the spiritual place he knew would be the perfect setting for his soul's returning. It had been so long since he had relinquished it.

If one read the scripts of religions, the mere idea of a life without a soul was unimaginable, the spiritual and the material tightly woven. Little did such scholarly minds know that one such as he had foregone the privilege of the soul. Handing it to another so very long ago: to the dybbuk who now waited in the rosewood box within the suitcase on the overhead baggage rack.

Around him, the travellers had changed several times. The child and his mother were elsewhere. But he knew their destination and it was perfect. Lochnagar, amidst isolated settlements where the winters would be harsh and bleak, farmsteads barricaded against the climate, whilst heaving penfolds of wintering livestock would provide perfect bone yards for his most remarkable constructs to date.

Things were gradually dovetailing, as he knew they would. The child. The time had finally come for the exchange.

A perfect, perfect sacrificial lamb.

VI

Thin Dust and Sadness

Glancing at her child beside her, suitcases sitting silently in the atrium lit by the dying sun that fell upon their tired shoes like sleep, she hesitated before opening the front door. Bottled window warping the interior hallway into dark, sloping shapes.

She found the light switch and the hallway softened. The solicitor had said he had arranged for the electricity and water to be reconnected in time for their arrival. She had no idea of the layout of the house. From the outside it looked haphazard, and she envisioned a warren of rooms, linked by doors and someone else's memories.

But tonight, she told herself firmly, they would only

need a bedroom, the kitchen and some way of running them both a bath.

To the left of the door, a large mirror reflected the staircase leading to the upper floors, unlit and waiting. Pictures and photographs lined the walls of the hallway and vast horns of trophy deer pricked the ceiling space. There were dressers and chairs pushed against the panelling. Some with dustcovers.

Some without.

Dark. That was her first impression. Dark and heavy, walnut and rosewood, deep red patterned paper on the walls and the unblinking glass eyes of the mummified trophies of past days of bullet and shot.

Duncan hung back, clutching her hand and burrowing in to her side. Usually so eager to explore, she had expected him to race down the corridor, up the stairs, to open closed doors, twisting keys, exclaiming. But instead he gazed up at her, eyes beseeching and his lip began to quiver, threatening tears.

"Let's leave the cases here, my pet, and go and find the kitchen. Perhaps it's that one?" pointing to a solitary door standing ajar at the farthest end of the hallway. "Shall we take a look?" He didn't smile. Perhaps he was as tired as she.

Together they walked slowly past the antlers of long-lost stags curled above them like a cruel canopy. Beneath the stuffed and mounted pheasants and foxes that had made shooting weekends at the lodge a profitable one.

Four other doors, set on opposite sides of the corridor, were closed. She had no desire to open them this evening;

they were both hungry and tired. Pushing the end door inwards they found themselves in a large kitchen, with a sash window that showed the dusk and a smudge of garden. They stood holding hands, feeling displaced and oddly anxious. She had known it would feel strange, but hadn't anticipated this unease. Perhaps if they had something warm inside them things would start to feel better.

"Let's find a kettle, a pan and some cups shall we?" Opening cupboards and drawers, Duncan found the kettle first whilst she located cups on a high shelf and gave them a rinse. She had filled a Thermos with milk before they left Newcastle. Duncan drew a chair to the table, resting his chin on his hands and smiled tiredly at her as she lit the gas ring with a taper.

"Cup of tea, and a piece of that lovely tiffin that Aunty Nora made."

Evening finally crept across the grass towards them; an early night it would have to be. After she had run him a hot bath. Leaving him to soak, she went and got a fresh towel from the suitcase and popped it on a chair next to him. The bathroom was next door to a large room that faced out across the front lawn and they could see the loch.

"We shall wake up to the sound of gulls," she said. The room needed an air, so she had opened the curtains and pushed up the casements. As she soaped the flannel to wash his back, weariness showed in his shoulders, and he was pulling on his ear like he had as a baby when sleep was needed.

She needed to find linen. Hoping it was dry after all these years. She hadn't thought about that when she had packed their suitcases. Theirs was coming in the large trunks that the stationmaster had said would be with them within the week.

In the hallway, behind yet another closed door, she located a set of shelves, stacked with sheets, pillowcases and blankets. Drawing them out she checked that they were dry and free of mold; there was a faint smell but it wasn't unpleasant. A hint of something. Mothballs? It made her smile as she pictured her mother-in-law carefully tucking them in between the cloth. The good thing was, she thought, the house would not present her with damp problems if these were still in good condition after all this time.

She made up their bed, rather hurriedly, not folding the corners properly, but what did it really matter? He wanted to sleep with her tonight, and she thought that was a lovely idea for both of them. The first night in a large and tired house. They could keep each other warm.

She realised she had left a case downstairs with their clothes in. He would need his pajamas. And she her nightgown and toiletries. As she reached the bottom of the stairs, calling to Duncan that she would be up to towel him dry in a matter of seconds, she noticed that the front door was ajar. Chiding herself for being thoughtless, she put the suitcase on the bottom step and moved across the hall to close the door. Tiredness, she thought, makes one forgetful. Tomorrow she would be more alert.

He was standing quite still in the shadows of the porch. She didn't have time to breathe or start in surprise. She didn't have time to back away. Through her panic she thought of her child upstairs. There was no phone line here, no one to call for help. Around her settled this dusty, lonely house and miles of emptiness. For those long seconds as she stared at him, she wondered for the first time since leaving London if this was madness.

He moved towards her into the light. She remained frozen to the spot. She couldn't breathe, and shock was making her hands tremble. As her hand went to her throat he said,

"I apologise for startling you. But the front door was open and I was directed here."

Seeing her bewilderment, "You do run a hotel?"

Her voice had disappeared and she stared at him, feeling the trembling take over her body. The voice of her child called down to her asking where she was – he was getting cold. The man turned to look in the direction of the voice and a smile appeared fleetingly on his lips.

She couldn't move, despite that terror that she felt. Her child. Could she manage to get to him in time? Was this stranger faster and stronger than her? Would she be overpowered just as she reached her child? And just as those infinite seconds threatened to ensnare her, the stranger coughed into a handkerchief. It snapped her back, as he said,

"Do you have a room for the night?"

As her eyes focused on the now, and the terror began to seep away she realised that there was something familiar about him. He was old, white hair beneath a cap, thick army surplus greatcoat across his arm. He looked tired. Not threatening now, just old and weary. His suitcase rested besides him, and she saw his shoes were dusty.

It was then she realised it was the elderly man her child had befriended on the train earlier that day. The chocolate man.

American chocolate.

Stepping closer, hesitation in his step and confusion upon his face, he held his hat like a supplicant between his fingers.

"Oh," she breathed. "You startled me. It's very late." Words rushed out of her. For in those seconds she had understood their very vulnerability here.

"Well… yes, we are opening an establishment. But we won't be open until the spring I'm afraid. We only arrived today. Did you walk here?"

Smiling, he bent to pick up his case. "I apologise. I alarmed you. I thought that the door was open for guests to register? You are not a hotel? Ah, then if you could kindly direct me to the village, I shall seek out a public house and a room for the night."

Flustered, she hesitated. Caught between this strange request and the voice of her child still calling. She answered and said she would be but a moment.

The old man had his suitcase in his hand and he bowed to her and said he would be on his way and that again he regretted startling her. As he turned and stepped back into the darkened atrium she remembered the story of the Good Samaritan. She had listened lovingly to those stories in the days when she had gone to church with her parents. Long-ago days, before the skies became loud with noises that never ended.

A stranger looking for a bed. She wouldn't turn guests away in the future, so perhaps, maybe, this was how it would be. But would he expect a fresh room? One with clean sheets and net curtains that gently blew. A small sachet of lavender in the wardrobe. A night-light so he could read. Breakfast. She had brought few provisions thinking that tomorrow they would explore the village. Just the two of them.

She had wanted, needed, to ease into this house, once the shining summer place for shooting parties, where pheasants would flutter in alarm as the dogs raced and the guns roared. A world of shooting sticks and late-night port, whilst the women waited.

They always waited, didn't they?

And now? Just a tired and old and empty house that she would have to work tirelessly to make into a hostelry. And a man seeking a bed for the night.

And so they remained. An odd late night tableau in the dim light of the hallway, hearing the child calling again, voice now high pitched and querulous. And her. Struggling between that powerful protective instinct and good manners, her exhaustion making split second decisions futile.

"Oh, hello sir. It is nice to see you again. Thank you very much for the chocolate. It was delicious. Mummy, can I have my pajamas please?" Standing on the small landing that split the staircase in two, he smiled at his mother and the old man. He had wrapped himself in the towel she had laid out. "Are you going to stay with us?"

His appearance shunted her into the present. Blushing at her awkwardness, she extended her hand to the man.

She could not possibly turn him away at this hour; that would be ill mannered of her. If he cared to stay here tonight, then tomorrow he could store his belongings here while he went and found premises in the village.

Feeling foolish, she apologised all the way up the stairs and onto the landing where she opened several doors until she found a room that looked suitable enough. The old man had followed her silently. Her child chattering away to the man about endless things that she didn't seem to hear. He placed his case upon the floor and smiled at her as she said she would go and find some bedding for him. As she closed the door to the room, he moved to the windows and looked out at a night that was now very dark. And yet he could see the shapes of the rocks against the sky, flat and rough. Allowing himself a small smile he patted the pocket of his coat as he lay it lovingly upon the unmade bed and whispered to the small construct that lay still and dormant.

"He truly is the perfect, perfect child."

Her child followed them into the kitchen. Dressing gown now wrapped around him. Pulling himself up to the table, he nibbled at a teacake with a small spread of jam and smiled at the man.

She wondered what to say to their lodger who sipped at his tea, eyes wandering around the kitchen, which she saw now was ageing and neglected and a rush of embarrassment blushed her cheeks.

Gone were her visions of rosy evenings that she had planned all these long months. Instead her tiredness sagged her and she saw merely the warped cupboards, smeared glass that should proudly show matching plates lined up on shelves, delicate cups and silverware. The walls were not covered with the paper of poppies and cornflowers that she had admired whilst out shopping with Nora; they were merely tired plaster-blackened with mold where the ceiling met the cornice.

The man was talking softly to Duncan... a strange lilt beneath the words, and she glanced to see her child pouring his tea into the saucer and blowing it gently to cool. Odd images of her Gordon, who had done this to amuse her, made her sadness spill over and she fought back the tears. It was the stranger that broke the moment as he said,

"I am sorry, once more, this disturbing of you. Thank you for tea and kindness. I shall retire to my room."

She put Duncan in bed, and went to fetch more linen. She would wash it all tomorrow and if the weather held, she would dry it outside in the garden. She had placed the old man in a room that was at the other end of the lodge to them despite the fact there were many rooms. She wasn't sure why that sub-conscious decision had been made despite her fluster and tiredness. But there was just something about the evening's events that made her lock their door.

Just to be on the safe side, Gordon.

And so it was for the man with the stolen teeth, and the lady with her lost youth and grief, that their night passed under a strange and unknown roof. Exhausted by so much, Annette fell asleep instantly, the warm body of her child curled up into a little ball next to her, soothed by his tiny breaths and dreaming mumbles.

*

Her watch showed 5 am. At some point their eiderdown had slipped to the floor, and her shoulders were chilled. Dawn wasn't far away, unlike sleep. Too restless to lie there, she rose, shrugging on a light gown and edged her feet into slippers.

Unoiled for years the door sighed with rust. Her child slept soundly though – like his father, little woke him. Not even the thud of the incendiary bombs in the London suburbs, so close to their Anderson shelter, had disturbed him.

The grandfather clock on the small landing, where the stairs twisted to the right, chimed as she descended the stairs. Sun and moon circling the face and the heavy hands swinging. Penduluming. Back and forth like the rhythmic suckling of a child. Soothing. But perhaps its hourly chimes had awoken her, leaving her with a mind too full of questions to wonder whose hand had wound it.

Following the curve of the stairs to the main hallway, past the doors that were locked and un-explored, into the echoing kitchen, vast ceilinged and draughty with that mould clutching peeling corners. It looked more forlorn this morning. Things she hadn't noticed last night now appeared. But her edginess had abated and she felt a tinge of anticipation at their new life.

In her head the faded plaster on the walls became fresh with coats of paint, dust covers lifted, heavy drapes thrown back so light could enter to welcome visitors. She would have to pace herself though. She would, in time, employ a maid and a gardener, but that would have to wait until after she had paying customers.

Guests would be entertained. She'd close part of this house off until she managed to let out the rooms when the weather brightened; for visitors who came here to walk loch shores and stride across the Cairngorms, picnicking by the dolmans that shouldered the weight of the weather today.

There would be tea on the lawn, like in the photograph. She had brought a few pictures of the lodge with her – indistinct and dark, taken by some unsure hand. In one, the lawn was occupied by a family sitting in wicker bucket chairs, occasional tables dotted with tea and cake stands. Whoever had been behind the lens had frozen this afternoon in a gentle moment before the skies burst and people were lost forever in someone else's war.

As dawn gradually lightened the room, she wandered into the open larder. Shelved to the ceiling. There was a small footstool to help her reach the uppermost heights. How sensible. One of the lower shelves contained cleaning products, and underneath it, on the tiled floor, a metal bucket and stiffened chamois leather. For how long they had been there she didn't care to question but they were still usable, she guessed. Apart from the leather whose journey would end in the fireplace, sending musky fumes up the flue.

Reading the labels carefully, she sorted them into those that would polish, those that would scrub and bleach, those that were for wood, those for tiles. Windows, she would use vinegar and newspaper.

Last night a lingering, unpleasant smell had caught her unawares, evident as they stepped into the hallway, less pungent in the upstairs rooms, but there nonetheless, like an afterthought beneath the surface. It was stronger in the kitchen this morning. Was it the drains or an outside issue? Perhaps the farms had been muck spreading. She knew little about the seasonal tasks linked with agriculture beyond creating a kitchen garden, and she wasn't in the least bit inclined to learn more!

Herbs though... to make sachets. Lavender and thyme. Come the spring, the garden would be a marvellous place for her to spend the afternoons before Duncan returned from the village school. She would pot out the crocuses, sow cottage flowers, and seed the vegetables. Hopefully the local grocery store would give her guidance about purchasing some hens and a cockerel. Noisy but necessary.

Little remained in the larder from the days when the house was a home; however, a few small jars set back against the wall revealed pickles and jams, dates obscured. In time she would easily fill the shelves. A visit to the village would be imminent. Nice walk for both of them. Later, when her boy awoke. Perhaps the old man could accompany them and then set off to find more permanent accommodation.

Wiping the surfaces with a cloth, years clung to the duster. It was a nice feeling though, this small gesture of ownership. Back and forth, back and forth. Towards the rear of the storage room, her foot touched something jutting out from under the base of the lower shelf where it adjoined the wall. Reaching down to stop it falling, she grasped the edge of a picture frame. Taking it to the window, she held it up to the light. Beneath the grime and smear, she saw patches of colour and gold leaf.

He was holding a lamb, whilst around his feet the whiteness of the adult flock mirrored his own gown. Staff in hand, the Highland valleys rolled away behind him to a loch that caught the sun.

"What a lovely omen... we shall place you above Duncan's bed. 'Suffer the little children to come to me.' How perfectly lovely and right."

Hearing Duncan call her name roused her from her reverie of sprigged wallpaper and cottage gardens. The larder was cleaned and she had found sets of crockery in the Welsh dresser. They were lovely. Patterns of flowers and fruit. They should be displayed. Soft oranges and pastel yellows.

Romance around the rim.

Smiling at her poetic moment, she went up to the bedroom and found him bleary-eyed and pale. He had his *Boy's Own Annual* open on his lap, small suitcase with his treasures neatly packed set on the side table.

"Shall we go and have breakfast my love?"

He smiled at her and said he was awfully hungry. He wondered what time the man would wake up.

"We'll let him wake up when he is ready, I think."

Together they went downstairs. He stopped a couple of

times to look more closely at a photograph or picture and remarked that he thought the stuffed and mounted heads were terrible things to do to an animal. She explained that this had been a hunting lodge when such things didn't worry people as much as they did these days.

"Before the war, Mummy?"

"Yes," she replied.

Before the war.

She made him a boiled egg, grateful for the fact that none had suffered on the journey from Newcastle, buttering the toast sparsely, cutting it into thin slices for dipping. Sitting next to him with her tea, she asked if he would like a walk to the village shop later so they could get supplies. He nodded, turning the eggshells over, pretending they were still whole. She would always feign shock at this and he would smile and say, "Not really Mummy!" Small moments of love and histories at their table. Their history would begin again here. One that Gordon would be proud of.

Ah, my dearest love. She had dreamt of him last night. Such a clear and lovely dream. She had heard his voice as though he were right beside her. Perhaps he had been. It left her with a fleeting comfort she hadn't felt since his death.

Pausing briefly outside the door of the old man's room she couldn't hear any signs of movement from within. Unsure as to what to do next, she decided that leaving him a note next to some sliced bread and an egg would be the most sensible. If he could leave the key under the statue of the faun on the front steps, she would let herself in.

When they had dressed and washed, she left the plates on the draining board to dry, propped the note against a cup and saucer on the kitchen table and picked up a sturdy basket from the larder shelf. Very useful for the shopping.

They took their hats in case the sun got too hot, and set off back down the driveway to the edge of the road, where the sign for Lochnagar pointed left. Braemar was a further ten miles northwest and another village name obscured by weather staining. Perhaps one day they would take a bus and explore. They'd find out the times. Duncan said he would like that, especially if there were deer on the Highlands instead of stuffed in their hall.

They walked beside the loch, taking in the vastness of it, flatly calm with a cloudless sky. A small island crowded with trees sat alone in the centre. No... there weren't any monsters beneath its surface, she assured him, but lots of fish. Trout indeed. And salmon.

There were two small boats that came with the house. Perfect for fishing trips. She presumed they were locked up safely in the boathouse. Yes she could row, but she would be much faster with him at the helm.

"Its correct name in Gaelic is Lochan na Gaire," she said as the road veered to the right and she could see the church steeple above poplars. "The 'little loch of the noisy sound', isn't that a lovely name?" Duncan smiled at the thought of water being too loud.

"And that summit there. You see it? Cac Càrn Beag."

He looked delighted and asked her where she had learnt that and she said she had found a book in the library when they had stayed with the Fosters. "So we have a good idea of where we are!"

Rounding the bend, the small town (no more than a hamlet) framed a village green with a pond in the centre. A post office sat next to a greengrocer's at the farthest end, a general store with its awning open, covering all manner of hardware and household necessities. The traditional public house sat beside the church.

"And there's my school Mummy."

There were a few people about. A man on a bicycle pedalling past a row of terraced cottages, a lady sitting near the pond with a book in her hands. There was an air of purpose that she found tranquil and comforting. Of things being settled, and the anxiousness of the night before seeping away.

"Which one shall we try first?" she asked, knowing that the greengrocer's may have sweets. Duncan pointed to it, taking in his surroundings and skipping occasionally. The lady who was reading her book turned to look at them and smiled, so they smiled back.

Walking into the shop, the air was cool and smelt of flour and chamomile. Behind the counter, shelves were stacked with tinned goods, and next to them a tall jar filled with sherbets and toffees. Duncan was mesmerised. In London, rationing had been so harsh there were rarely any sweets available. And if there were, the cost of them was shocking.

Annette took out her shopping list and then introduced themselves, explaining where they were now living and saw a sudden interest in the eyes of the woman behind the counter.

"What a lovely lady she was. Quiet and very house proud. We would see her at the kirk of course. Sundays. Evensong usually. Lived here for years with her lad until he moved south to the city." Grand that the house would be lived in again. Wasn't right that it had stood empty for so long.

Annette smiled and said she would have loved to have known her and the conversation veered towards more mundane issues.

These are made hereabouts. The toffees. Would the wee man like a sherbet? How were they settling in? Happy to continue in this vein, Annette asked about help around the house, a gardener and a handyman. In time, someone who could live in during the week?

Oh yes indeed, she knew some fine young girls with wonderful references hereabouts. They would all be in the church this coming Sunday, would she like an introduction? Did she know where the church was? She would be welcomed with open arms if they could make it.

Annette thanked her and said yes, they were churchgoers. Duncan happily sucked his sweets with several more in his pocket for after lunch as she read out the items from her shopping list, apologising that there was not too much today as they had to carry it all back. Staples such as eggs, butter, flour. Some vegetables and a query about chickens.

"We would love to have our own eggs," she said, and the woman gave her the name of a local farmer who would sell her some very reasonably. Seed packets of vegetables and herbs completed her order and they happily trundled back up the hill to admire their purchases.

"She was a nice woman, wasn't she Mummy?" She was, said Annette. To be honest, she had been worried that their arrival would cause suspicion within such a close-knit community. That they would be treated with caution. But this hadn't been the case today. Gordon's mother had in her own way made sure they were welcomed.

As their loch view appeared, the noise of a car approached them from behind; grasping her child's hand Annette moved them next to the hedge border. Slowing down, a male voice called out.

"Hello there! Care for a lift?"

Mustachioed and smiling, he leant through the car window. Tweed cap pulled down over his brow and dark sunglasses masking his eyes. There was a large mole on his right cheek. Taken aback, she thanked him and explained they were very nearly home.

"Oh come now, surely a gentleman can offer his services to an attractive lady and child? After all, that's what neighbours are for."

"Thank you again, but we are very nearly home." She had set her bags down. "We are just up the hill to the right. Beyond the loch."

"Yes I believe so. Small world. News travels and all that. Hop in. I insist," he said and stepped out, gathered their shopping and placed it in the boot.

Hesitating, Annette realised that it was now impossible to refuse without appearing terribly rude. Still, she felt it was very presumptuous of him, albeit there were obviously good intentions in his offer. Duncan climbed into the back of the car with her. He said he liked the car and were the seats leather?

"Indeed they are young man."

Introducing himself as Major Evelyn, George Evelyn, how do you do, Duncan asked him where he was from. They were from London.

"Cheltenham, my boy. Came up here for the grouse season. Stayed. Marvellous place. Air you know, plenty of shooting." He smiled at him in the mirror.

Clasping Duncan's hand, Annette leant forward. "It's just over here, to the right. Thank you. Very kind of you."

"How about I drive you right up the door and then you can invite me in for a cup of tea?"

Annette hesitated. First the old man appearing unexpectedly and now this. The house was hardly a home, let alone a hotel. She wasn't in the habit of inviting strangers in and yet she had last night, and she really didn't know what to say. There was something in his manner that was far too familiar. An intimacy not invited. It made her feel uncomfortable, intruded upon. She said finally, "I am awfully sorry, but we have just moved in, and the house really isn't in a fit state for visitors."

"Oh don't worry about that. I'll help you in with the shopping, and be gone before you know it." Duncan nipped out to open the gate and then followed the car up the drive to the front door.

"Splendid house this," remarked the Major, "lovely views." His eyes lingered on her body and the hand on the small of her back stayed for just a few seconds too long.

Awkwardly, Annette led them into the house, where the Major placed the shopping on the kitchen table. Acutely aware yet again of the tell-tale signs of neglect and time, she occupied herself with putting on the kettle and getting cups and the teapot ready, wondering how long he would insist on staying and what on earth she would say to the man.

Pulling up a chair, he sat down and looked around. Conversation appeared to be a gift for him, and she imagined he would be at ease anywhere. War made people resilient. Social order had been re-adjusted. There were no longer the class issues of the pre-war years. Still, she felt uncomfortable in his presence and hoped he would have the good manners and grace to leave as soon as he had had his tea.

Duncan had gone to his bedroom, hurrying back, carrying his collection of small model planes. He spread them on the table, questioning the man about them, their names, and dates of manufacture. Mentioning his daddy was in the RAF. Had the major been a pilot? Had he flown bombers?

No, he had been in the navy. A lieutenant commander, no less. But such a title was a bit of a mouthful for people around here to say, so he settled for Major instead. Duncan looked suitably impressed. Annette thought him rude. And condescending.

Pouring the tea, Annette was glad that she didn't have to talk to this man. Her child was deep in conversations about planes and ships, and she allowed her mind to drift to the last letter that she had received from Gordon before the awful telegram.

VII

The Clockmaker

They knew it was over. Him and his co-workers. That final day. For on that day no one came to take them from their cells. The corridors beyond their separate units were silent of the sounds of feet, of voices raised in harsh Germanic tones. This silence confused him.

For years he had been assaulted by the noise of this place. The arrogance and brutality of the guards. The warped visions of Hitler. Never to begin another day of shame chained to the bench in a lab or workshop. Morse messages tapped along the pipes of their cells with tin cups and fingernails. Hopes and dreams of rescues and freedoms, of Americans and Russians with door keys and handshakes.

Unfortunately for the Clockmaker, freedom wore a different guise. Munitions fell, bright flashes through his barred window. He did not know if they were bombs or shells. Only that one minute he was peering through the bars at another firestorm, yet more wounds burned into the flesh of the city. The next thing he knew, he was waking under a cairn of rubble – his flesh torn and open, wounds that would have killed another man. But he was not as other men. It was not his fate to die by an artifice devised by human hands. The Nazis had discovered that fact, deep within the torture dungeons soon after they had found him. And so had he. It's quite a thing to find out that you do not die no matter how your body is sliced, burnt or stabbed. That your body will heal in time from such cruel hurt inflicted upon it by others.

The same could not be said of his soul. A soul that should be nourished by the joy of children at his clever toys. By the way his wondrous clocks, brightly painted works of art, would delight their owners as pairs of waltzing figures or rotating birds announced the passing of time. A soul at peace with its place in the world. Not his. *Not his.*

Then the Führer found him. He stood in the Clockmaker's chamber, gazing at all the things created from the bones of rodents, piano wire and even his own hair. They dragged him kicking and screaming into a world of war, death and pain. Soldiers ordered to press burning iron into his flesh, abusing his body to learn his secrets, then ultimately enslave his genius until a more fitting use could be found for him. With each cut of a blade, each burning torment a tiny light in his soul went out to be replaced by the cold voids of the dark.

His airways choked with dust. Each breath a conflict. With shaking fingers, broken and bloody stone by stone, he painstakingly cleared the rubble from his body. Until he finally rose from the debris and stood on unsteady legs. The wall of his cell was no longer there.

He did not know how much time had passed since the onslaught had begun. But dust and smoke still hung in the air of his cell. Suspended, unmoving, a snapshot in time. As if the city itself held its breath at the passing of the world's latest warmonger and the fall of his Third Reich.

The staccato rattle of gunfire reached him from far across the city. He listened for a moment. It appeared distant, but the Clockmaker knew not to totally trust his hearing. This ruin of a city could dampen or echo sounds with ease. He did not recognise the weapons' bark and decided to presume it was not German fingers pulling the triggers. Time to move.

Quickly he found his secret hiding place amongst the rubble – a loose stone slab on his cell floor, beneath which he had dug a pit that he used to hide stolen objects that would serve him well. It had been easy enough to do, a spoon to dig with; spreading the unearthed grit and dirt about his cell's floor.

Nobody paid attention to the condition of a cell belonging to an unkempt old man. He cleared away the dust and the debris and with prising fingers eased it clear to reveal his collection wrapped within a rough sack.

Carefully, he lifted it from his hiding place. With gentle hands he removed its content and ran loving fingers over the cover of an ancient book, far older than he. His fingertips brushed over the ridged surface, ribbed and wrinkled like the bark of an old tree. It was made of thin hide or leather of the darkest brown. On his darker days he wondered if it was actually animal hide or not. No words adorned the cover to label the tome or hint at its purpose. But inside on curled, yellowing pages of thick vellum, words from a language he had only begun to understand were written in thin, red watery ink. They continued for only a third of the book, then abruptly stopped, leaving the rest of the pages blank. A mystery he took upon himself to solve.

He had discovered the book when researching information on one of the projects he had been forced to work on. There was much about this new world that he did not yet understand. And as he searched through the extensive archives of his captives, he stumbled across some of Hitler's collection of occult curios. It had been insinuated that the Nazi Party grew from occult groups. Adapting religious symbols for their own devices. The swastika – the Hindu symbol for the sun.

Hitler sent his minions out into the world to find items and books of religious or occult symbolism; items that would bring him power and bring his dreams to fruition. The Clockmaker had found so many within the libraries of the underground chambers. When he could, he would visit them, furtively taking a book or scroll to pore over.

Towards the end, none of the guards took notice of this bent old man shuffling up and down the corridors at a glacial pace, with stacks of books or scrolls under his arm as he went about his work. For they had far greater concerns as the bombs and shells dropped increasingly closer and the ravings of their ailing leader got ever wilder. They would huddle in whispering corners in ones and twos or just stare out blankly with glass doll eyes from haunted faces. As he passed them he would wonder what inner turmoil was boiling the minds behind those eyes. Was the foot soldier truly to blame for his actions while wearing the uniform of the Wehrmacht? Perhaps they had been as he once was, the maker of clocks or perhaps they tilled the earth or kept the shop. Had they flocked to the Führer's banner or were they dragged? Did they wish, as they had stood guard over their leader, they had pulled their pistol, placed it to his temple – shaking finger on the trigger and simply shot him?

Would he have done so if he had stood in their shoes – could he have? To end it all before so much death, pain and misery been inflicted on the world. Or perhaps it was simply easier to have regrets when the wolves were scratching at the bunker door. He shook the thoughts away. The time for contemplation was later.

Reaching into the sack he found the small rosewood box. A curious item of ancient Hebraic origin found next to the book. Ah... Kabbalah, with your demons and dybbuks. Bridges between deity and infinity. Evil was an illusion they preached, demons that sit in their thousands upon the left and right hands of mortal men. But this?

He opened the lid to check its content. Inside was a tiny little humanoid corpse, perfectly preserved as if mummified.

Its wrinkled skin was a pale blue colour covered in tiny, downy hairs. Above the eyes, sealed tightly shut, were the tiny nubs of a pair of horns. He had no idea of what it was, some kind of elf, fairy or imp or just a freak of nature. He was sure the book referred to it, some kind of journal perhaps chronicling its discovery or clues to its identity.

Also in the sack were strips of cloth, a spoon and some surgical spirit; tweezers, pliers and miniature screwdrivers pilfered from a workbench. He used the spirit to cleanse his wounds and dressed them as best he could with the cloth. Clutching the sack he stepped through the ruin of his cell wall into freedom. Behind him he could hear the muffled cries of the trapped and the dying, the yells and cries of victors poring over their spoils. He picked his way through the outer rubble of his prison and ran.

VIII

Newness

Annette entered the village post office and joined the queue. It was rather long but she was in no rush. She had accompanied Duncan to his first day at the church school. He was excited, he said, and wanted to make new friends that he could bring back to Loch House and play with. His hair looked sharp, he said, and she smiled and asked where had he learnt that phrase? His satchel was polished and the pencils the Fosters had given him were in there, together with a ledger and his sandwiches.

The teacher had met them at the door, an older man, whom she suspected was ex-army. Other children flocked in beside Duncan, taking curious glances at him. One boy had stopped and said "Hello". She left him smiling as he mounted the steps into the building. Fretting slightly, she thought her day's chores would take her mind off the anxieties of him settling in. Besides, she would make a Victoria sponge cake for him on his return, and then they would walk along the loch side before bed.

She should have known better. Friday morning. There was bound to be a long line of customers. She had written a thank you letter to the Fosters for their hospitality, although it was far more than that, but she couldn't find the words, and enclosed an oat biscuit recipe for Nora. She must remember to buy several stamps at once to keep in the writing bureau she had seen in one of the empty rooms. She would get it moved to her room in time. It was a lovely oak with a folding table and numerous drawers for stationery.

It wasn't cold out but she had decided to wear the cardigan she had knitted for Gordon. It was from a pattern a neighbour had given her; she had made quite a good job of it – even if she said so herself. It was navy with large, brown wooden buttons. He had looked quite fetching in it. It was far too big for her but when she wrapped herself within it and rested her cheek on the high collar, she could still smell him.

The post office, it transpired, was the place where the village gossip was updated, a daily pastime, wiling away the minutes as the old man behind the counter fumbled with slips of paper, stamps and coins. Why were post offices always staffed by the elderly, she wondered? Perhaps to allow the gossips time to spread their tales?

The shop was small, its shelves and displays fairly threadbare; she could only examine their meagre contents or check the address on her envelope so many times before she inevitably tuned into the gossip of the day. Of the two ladies directly in front of her, she knew neither. One was a smallish woman, plump, squeezed into a white blouse and long dark skirt; her accent was thick, Glasgow perhaps, a little common. Harsh.

The other was slender. A good few inches taller than she. The polar opposite to the other. She wore a long coat, tailored, expensive, matching dark brown skirt and hat, a little too dressy for the village, she thought. County, not town. Annette wondered where she lived.

"Hen saw him last night," the smaller lady told her disapprovingly. "Drunk as a lord he was, dressed in some long black robe. Martins' Harlequins ball no doubt, staggering around like some newborn he was. Considering he was Navy. Or so he says!"

The taller woman tutted. "Well I was at the Martins' party and I for one never saw him, nor anyone dressed like that. Odd choice."

"Well I wouldn't know, the likes of us are not invited," the other huffed as she crossed her arms and pushed up her bosom. Annette thought for a moment that the blouse might not survive.

"Really? Well I am surprised. It was a fabulous do, considering." Her sentence faltered at the appearance of Major Evelyn. The patter of gossip subsided as all eyes in the queue turned to him. There was a frisson of discomfort from the two women in front of her and Annette realised they must have been discussing him. She hadn't seen him since the day he had offered them a lift, and suddenly wished she were elsewhere.

He was wearing a smart tweed suit, lifting his cap in greeting to the women in the line. The two women in front of her nodded, exchanging glances. Noticing Annette, he stepped swiftly forward and stood beside her, offering his hand. Annette took it out of politeness, withdrawing hers as he held it for longer than was appropriate.

"How are you settling in?"

Things were beginning to be organised she said, aware that ears were tuned in to this exchange, and he smiled and said good, then he would pop over for a cup of tea in the next couple of days. She didn't reply and desperately wished the gentleman behind the counter would hurry up so she could escape from this queue.

Evelyn drawled loudly, "Poorest service I have ever come across. Typical backwater village! Hurry up down there, man." The postmaster had either not heard the loud comments, or simply ignored the brash rudeness of the man.

Shocked, Annette glanced at the women in front of her whose shoulders had stiffened at his remarks but they too said nothing. *What an awful man*, she thought, uneasiness overwhelming her, so she excused herself, and left the shop.

Hurrying across the green she passed by the memorial for those who had made the ultimate sacrifice during the Great War. Names carved into the grey stone column. The list was not long, but the names carved there were still too many. She paused to look at the flowers gently propped against the plinth and her thoughts turned to the days after the telegram had arrived.

More names to be added from this war.

Wrapping herself in the cardigan, her thoughts flowed into the time they had spent with the Fosters in Newcastle. They had asked her to come and stay. Help her to get through that awful time. And they had. In so many small and magical ways.

*

The giddy laughter as Walter paraded in front of the children in his wife's best hat. The games he played with little Anne, the knocks on the door as her father returned from war. *Oh Gordon.* Perhaps it was where she sat that brought back the pain, brought back the tears. Sat before a monument to the fallen, it was bound to happen. Her mind pictured Gordon old and grey answering questions about trains to eager grandchildren. To playing games with Duncan; the knocking on the door of a returning father.

Those summer weeks spent with Walter and Nora, daughter Anne. Uncle and Aunty. Although they had been on Gordon's side of the family they had embraced her and his child as their own.

A family of war heroes, chest full of medals, recognition for six years of service in the many fields of battle. North Africa, at El Alamein he was there – Italy too. Walter had met the Pope once, gave him a bottle of wine he did. He must have blessed it; for unlike far too many, return Walter did.

Skin like leather even now, tanned by years of foreign suns. His hair thinned, but he had kept his looks. Piercing blue eyes that held court to children sitting crossed-legged in a row, demanding stories of glories past. Anne, cousins, children from the street, Duncan. Never far from Anne's side. Annette would listen too; they all did in muted excitement. She admired how he did it, how he spun the tales and truths suitable for the ears of children who never grew tired of the telling.

Months had rolled into a year or more since Berlin had fallen. Walter had resisted speaking of the sights those blue eyes had seen. But as time passed, his tongue had been loosened in a way that only an insistent audience of eager children could. But there were moments, away from the innocence of children, that Annette saw his face cloud with the passing shadows of remembrance; friends lost, horrors witnessed. But as soon as they appeared, they would be dispelled by the laughter of the very young and the very living. After all, it was for them, for their here, their now and their tomorrows.

Annette smiled to herself as she heard the echoes of the children, as Walter entered a room wearing Nora's latest hat of high fashion, a milliner in Bainbridge. As a couple they were wonderful together. Anne had inherited the best of both of them, hair black as a raven, just like her mother, and irises of cloudless skies. She would persuade her father to go outside and knock on the front door, the children sitting on the stairs eagerly waiting. Then running down the hall she would reach and open the door, and again be the first to set eyes on her soldier returning home.

Annette would watch these precious moments, never fully able to share in the joy. For Duncan never had his chance to run down a corridor. Gordon, husband and father never returned to knock on their door. It remained closed, lost. Walter understood. He would pass with Anne upon his shoulders, pausing to place a hand upon her shoulder.

Warm love and laughter. Those were words linked with the Fosters. It was as if someone had trapped a piece of sunshine, wrapped it in bricks and mortar and carefully placed it on Chillingham Road.

There were others too of course. Brian and Derek, cousins to little Anne. They were a decade or so older than Duncan, young men starting to make their way in the world, becoming quite the men about town. They would take Duncan to the city, the Tyne, the shipyards, how he loved that. But it was Anne he adored. Shadowing her heels as they ran through the park at the end of the street. Hiding in the mazes and below the bridges.

Their last day had been glorious. Picnic in Jesmond Park. They had all gone. Friends, cousins, her new family. The place was full to bursting. It was as if half of Newcastle was there. The sun high and hot. It brought out the colours of the hedges and blooms and filled the park with such scents. Nora had put on such a spread with cakes, so many cakes. Annette often wondered where she got it all from, or the ingredients to bake it, but she thought it best not to ask.

Then fond farewells, sadness for Annette and her child. Some of the wounds of losing had begun to heal. She would miss them, would they come and visit once the house was ready? They would. Duncan begged that it would be soon and Anne linked her little finger with his and smiled, and he knew it would be.

Their future was away in the distance – running ahead like the iron tracks through Northumberland… all the way home.

To Scotland.

IX

Berlin

Berlin was a hellscape. A nightmare made real. A place of darkness and eternal shadow. Ash fell like snow, covering the living and the dead. It was no longer a city. Twisted girders and the skeletons of once proud buildings pointed defeated fingers towards the Allies. Such was the smoke and soot, that the sun no longer moved across the sky, unable to gaze upon the devastation humanity visited upon itself. Had the city surrendered? The rumble of war still reached him from the western edges of the city. Were the remnants of Berlin's defenders attempting to break out of a city choked in the iron grip of Soviet Russia falling into the softer hands of the Western Allies?

The Clockmaker knew to head north. Carefully he moved from shadow to shadow, treasures slung in a makeshift tote across his back. Passing amongst the shadows, listening for warning signs, shifts and footfalls upon the debris. Hidden by the smog he hurried forwards. Hearing voices he would cover himself in debris, no one noticed another pile of rags amongst so many fallen. Only the animals would come and disturb him. No food was left in the city, but vermin must eat. Animals scoured the alleys and fallen buildings in packs, competing with roving bands of men desperate to flee the city. But it seemed only the animals were gaining weight. For the eaters of the dead and dying, of those too weak to fight back, it was a bountiful harvest. He began to pass the first bodies. Isolated. Sparse clumps of rags and shadow marking the fallen.

Smoke, oil and spoiling meat flavoured the air now. Shell holes, walls, makeshift barricades trapped sprawling figures, the human litter of the Red Army's offensive. Burnt-out vehicles charted its advance, broken artillery piece bowing its head in submission. But he was not the only traveller. Many were afoot.

Progress was slow as he tried as best he could to move parallel to the main arteries out of the dead heart of the city. Shadows swung from the lampposts, boards around their necks branding them traitors, communists. Some hung limply, knots tied by Soviet hands.

Bands of victorious soldiers meandered drunkenly through the streets; he hid from them too. They frightened him more than the guards who had tortured him. For at least he knew their intent. These gross men. They frightened him. Unsure of their purpose. He was sure to them he would sound like the enemy. For what was he? Neither Russian, nor German but he could speak it and he certainly couldn't pass for an American. A flat line refugee.

So he hid. Cleaning his wounds daily with surgical spirit and cloth stolen from the bunker. Cover was easier to find as he moved towards Berlin's outskirts. Buildings more intact. Some of the houses still bore Goebbel's appeals for the citizens of Berlin to rise up and halt the enemy at the gates, scrawled across their brickwork in white paint.

Occasionally he would find a stone shell to rest in, to hide in, away from the shadows and the voices.

Until one day his luck ran out.

Sharp pain wrenched him from unsettled dreams of death and pain. He awoke to find himself staring at the point of a steel bayonet and into the eyes of a dark-haired youth clad in the uniform of Comrade Stalin's Red Army. Harsh words spat at him in a language he could not possibly understand. But the meaning was clear. He was beckoned to stand and he did unsteadily, holding his side where the wound was still healing.

The boy thrust a rifle butt between his ribs and he groaned in pain and swore in German. Too late through the haze of shock and pain did he realise his mistake. The youth smilingly pulled the trigger, and pain lanced through the old man's side. Looking down at the spray of blood now decorating his rags, he swallowed that cry of pain with gritted teeth, anger boiling within him.

Once too often in this city, his flesh had been violated. A final thread of restraint snapped as he looked at the Russian and smiled. Standing his ground against the waves of agony. He would not fall, not even for a second, as his freedom whispered of lands beyond the seas that he would head for. Where he would summon them.

His constructs.

His way out of this world, of these endless lives.

Wild-eyed and panicking, the youth scrambled for his trigger, a hollow click of the Red Army's depleted ammunition sealed this young man's fate. Realisation crept across his features, as he backed away, panicked and defeated. The Clockmaker sprang. Falling upon the young man. Mere inches taller than the Soviet, the Führer had kept him well fed to the end, ensuring that starving bellies never distracted his creators from their work.

Pinning the half-starved youth to the ground he turned the blade, level with the heart of his victim and pushed. Shrieking, his voice echoed around the enclosed walls of this ruination of a house, and he squirmed beneath the older man, fighting with all his might. He spat into the face of the old man as the blade point pierced the cloth of his uniform and began to dig through his skin. He shrieked in pain and thrashed his limbs wildly as the blade bore through bone, curses became sobs or perhaps pleadings for life as the blade scratched cardiac tissue, his words lost on the old man, at this point there was no turning back, death an inevitability. Eventually the youth, exhausted by the toil of months and the strength of this frail-looking elderly man, ceased his struggling.

The old man looked into the youth's eyes as he stole all his tomorrows and those of children he would never bring into the world. And with each moment the blade eagerly opened his heart, the young man stared at the Clockmaker until the light of his life finally went out with a sigh of

"*Mama*".

Welcoming the seeping blood of the youth to warm his bones, the city was silent beyond him. Struck momentarily by how peaceful he felt as he lay upon the corpse; it was calming to absorb its warmth.

Sagging with exhaustion, he glanced down at the corpse below him. The head had rolled back, tongue lolled to the side of an open mouth, untarnished teeth, arms spread wide in cruciform. The dagger still sunk deep into his chest, a dull metal island in a lake of crimson. Piling the soldier's clothes to one side, he selected the boots and greatcoat.

The man was thin, brittle. Raised cords of muscle and tendon on his forearms pitted with fissures and scars. The Clockmaker looked more closely at the young man's body. As he ran a thick tongue along his gum line emptied by the endless questings of Nazi pliers, he thought they reminded him of the wires and strips of cat gut he had used to form his automations, lovingly constructed before the Führer had found him. How soon before the packs of animals discovered his scent? Tearing the bayonet from the ravaged heart, he dragged the body into the next room.

It was that night with the stench of his first murder

clinging to him like a shroud, that the little creature in the rosewood box first visited him in dreams. He found himself looking into oval eyes which were no longer sealed shut. The tiny horns curled back across its skull were ridged and cream. In his nightmare it hovered about his face, extending slender claws to touch his mouth. He whispered and questioned its being. Asked for a name, a title. The blue halo shivered around it and he strained to hear the word it uttered.

Waking lathered in sweat, cold fear in his heart, he turned onto his side and tried to breathe calmly. Lighting a nub of a candle with one of his last remaining matches, he listened for the sounds of the city and the night. It was quieter than he had known it. He felt neither hunger nor thirst. His wounds ached but he knew they would heal in days and he would be strong enough to continue his final journey.

The book lay next to him although he could not recall leaving it there. Its cover now stained in Russian blood. With shaking apprehensive hands he opened it. It had changed. Empty pages no longer blank. Under the flickering flame of the candle, swirling words danced across more of the pages. The light was weak and his eyesight not as strong as in the past. Perhaps written by the same hand, with ink of a much deeper hue. Red words that made sounds he had never before heard, that his tongue found difficult to articulate, words that somehow, he understood.

Each night within that shell of a building he would be visited by dreams of far-off lands, of deserts, and mountain ranges of sand. Ancient symbols and hidden places. The last image he would remember as he woke would be a narrow pair of smiling amber eyes. No more words would appear on the pages, even though there were still so many to fill. With each passing night he could understand a little bit more of their meaning as the deep red writing began to fade into the watery original. He began to realise the message of the book was incomplete.

His days belonged to endless trudging, hiding and foraging for food. He was not sure of the direction he was travelling any more, the book's mystery occupying his waking thoughts, tugging at his imagination, calling to the academic in him, the engineer, the artist, the intelligence that needed to grasp this. At night he would turn in early, rushing into the warm embrace of those small amber eyes and where they might take him.

To places. Dark places. Remembering the catacombs in frozen Siberia. Deep within the earth he had travelled. Along passageways inscribed with terrible hieroglyphs – speaking of things he never wished to understand. He remembered feeling the things that dwelt there. Terrible intelligences, ancient things that lived in the dark. Forms with claws and hungry maws of teeth that would not just pierce this body, but hungered for the souls of men. A vast consciousness that he could feel pressing down on him, suffocating him as if he was being physically absorbed by something so evil it probed to find the tiniest fissure in which to enter his mind.

And consume him.

He recalled the dreams as vividly as if he had walked the passageways himself. How he had stood at a crossroads of tunnels before a giant stone door. Strange symbols, worn to be almost indistinguishable by the passage of the ages, writhed and writhed across its surface.

Where the door met the dust of the floor, a small crack meandered up its surface. He felt the minds behind the door calling to him; prise open the crack so they could see light again after being trapped in the dark for so very, very long. He had watched his shadow dance in the light of the torch flame he carried. As if in time to the breathing of those behind the door.

His shadow had flickered and left him fleeing along the passageways. His very soul had torn itself from its prison of flesh and fled in revulsion from the place in which his body had carried it. He had chased it and found the tunnel led out into the sunlight. He did not return.

He had dreamt of other places. Of ancient times, where the power of the earth was revered and had been called upon to release its bounty, offering its peoples a plentiful harvest among other things. Of standing stones and ancient power. Places of power held in check, barred from the world by an ancient wall built long ago by a long-dead empire. A place too far north to feel the despoiling kiss of the standards topped with golden eagles.

Beyond the reach of the Caesars, the Bonaparte and the führers.

X

Annette

That night, once she had cleared the plates away, and settled her son in his bed, tales of his day and new friends had tired him, she found she was too restless for sleep or for reading her book. The house was quiet, surrounded by the sound of the loch against the shores. No foxes barked, nor owls called for their mates. There was little wind in the pines, and it was too dark to see if mist had settled on the rims of the Cairngorms. What a strange journey had led them here. One of grief and absence. One of new beginnings.

Her slippers felt thin as she mounted the stairs to the upper storey of the house, treads edgy beneath her feet as she switched on the lights. The switch was round and warm to her touch, button flicks before the landing light hesitated and came on. A single bulb. No lampshade. Which was odd. She had the feeling that Gordon's mother had been fastidious about such details. The landing stretched the width of the lodge. Not straight, as the wings to the side of the house jutted out at the front, with large bay windowed rooms she hadn't yet opened or aired.

There were sets of doors on either side. For storage she suspected, or for days long ago when such houses had servants who lived in. Before they marched to war and the trenches. And never returned. Leaving sisters, wives, and sweethearts.

Her hand went to her throat as the grief caught in her heart and threatened to pour out again. Distracting her. Opening the first of many doors, she lit the room and saw shapes beneath dustsheets. Removing them, the dust settled around her. There were chairs, bent-backed and oak that would be fine for the kitchen. Chests of drawers too heavy for her to lift on her own, but with help they could be restored and placed into guest rooms. Polished to a rosewood shine. Folding the dustsheets into neat squares she made a mental note to wash them. Spreading them freshly onto the clothesline to dry crisp in the summer sun. She would iron them and starch them. Packing them into the large airing room. Matching pillowcases and bedspreads. Sprigs of lavender perhaps.

For luck and love.

Room after room contained treasures of past lives. Ornaments, mirrors, perched on shelves and nestled in boxes and hampers. Toys of children who had played in the rooms and beyond in the streams and hills. A train set that would have been her beloved Gordon's, and that his only child would now play with. Tracks winding between wooden villages. Stiff trees pricking up between shops and tiny lead figures at stations and post offices. She found an empty box between some chairs, and using one of the dustsheets, began to wrap the small Hornby locomotives carefully. Brown carriages, and dark green engines, tiny wheels that would run along tracks, die-cast metal and journeys.

He could help her take the large wooden landscaped board down the stairs. The track firmly pinned in place. The loch and the house at the end of the line. Hills and tunnels, gorse and small miniature deer dotted the flanks of the mountains.

She marvelled at the workmanship, lovingly painted, set down in their forever places. Locomotives pulling carriages much like the one they had travelled in, sidings where containers were piled with coal, bobbly to the touch. And here, right in the heart of the railway world was their own house. So detailed it could have been shrunk and set down brick by brick. If she peeked closely would she see herself peering out through the dormer window? And that made her smile.

Glancing at her watch she realised that it was five in the morning.

Annette drew open the drapes in the front parlour, pushing the large doors open to let air into the room. You could step straight out onto the terrace that was covered by a sloping roof supported by trellised columns. Ideal. For tea. Even if it rained. Which of course it would do many times in the year.

The velvet and lining was stiff with dust and she wondered whether she should take them down and air them. They would be heavy and cumbersome though. Beyond the doors the dawn had finally appeared and it softened the mountains and lent a gentle tint to the loch's icy waters. She could hear the water against the shore, the breeze picking up in the lavender and some unnamed birdsong far away.

Standing there in her slippers and thin gown, she felt a release of something. Intangible and fragile. It made her recall a book her grandmother had given her. Of a peaceful child with golden locks, dressed as a fairy, sitting on the steps as her parents held a carnival ball. She had envied the child the curls and the wings.

The kettle had boiled and she sat at the table listening to the stillness. It would take some getting used to, this lack of sound. London had been noise. You grew accustomed to it until sometimes you weren't aware of it. She thought she would always notice the silence here, though. Pulling herself from her reverie she decided to try and make the kitchen more habitable.

Satisfied that her dusting skills had not been in vain, she placed the crockery neatly on the shelves of the large cupboards. The glass gleamed now. She had used a mixture of soda and vinegar. Both had been easy to get after the war. And wiped any smears away with newspaper.

It was a beautiful set of china. Small blue and orange flowers – some of them cornflowers – others she couldn't name, arranged in clusters around the rims of the plates and the cups and the bowls. The large dinner plates she set on the topmost shelf which was high and so she had stood on a chair to save chipping or dropping them.

On the next shelf came the side plates, and then lower down the dessert bowls and teacups. And finally on the wide surface of the dresser she placed the serving tureens and platters. They would look so fine as she placed the food on the tables for the guests she hoped would frequent her guesthouse in the warmer weather.

There were cupboards she hadn't opened yet. The cellar, the far reaches of the house. And for an instant the weight of responsibility clouded her moments of delight. Perhaps she would bake oatcakes and warm bread. And make soup. It would be wonderful to restore the vegetable garden. It was neatly walled and the stakes for peas and beans still standing straight despite the winds that would race down the valleys and across the loch towards this house.

She had been awake most of the night but didn't feel tired. She would make a cup of hot cocoa and go and wake her tousled-haired lad in a while. Taking her apron off, and picking up her cup, she stepped out into the kitchen garden. She would replace the soil path with flagstones, plant borders of annual flowers alongside it, all the way to where it ended at the stream. Beyond the water, the hill rose steeply, topped by an old barn with a domed roof. Weathered and wooden, she liked the fact that it seemed to belong to its surroundings. They would too in time.

To her left there was a birdbath, greened and furrowed by damp and small things that grew upon stone. It was pretty. Dawn had lapsed into an early morning. She liked the fact she had accomplished so much. Wandering around the back she turned the corner to the front of the house. It was nice to stroll.

Beneath the window of what would be the dining room, she hoped, there was another of the faun statues. He was standing on one leg and playing his flute with a look of mischief upon his face. They popped up everywhere it would seem. Small ornaments of him, a rug tightly embroidered and red with the gold of his panpipe slightly faded. She was quite sure there were others but they hadn't found them yet. It was like a treasure hunt.

She recalled a lovely fable she once read. A satyr came across a traveller wandering in the forests in the depths of winter. Taking pity on him, the satyr invited him into his home. It was small and crowded with animals. She often wondered why a faun would live in a house rather than a cave. But never mind.

The faun made the traveller some soup in a large tureen over an open fire. In the tale, the man kept blowing on his fingers, when the satyr asked him what he was doing the traveller said it was to keep him warm. Sitting down at the table, the man blew on his soup saying this was to cool it; the honest woodland creature is appalled at such double-dealing and drives the traveller back into the woods.

After breakfast Duncan said he had invited a boy to come and play. He was nice and his name was Albert. He was in the same class and liked planes. He was also very good at spelling. Was it okay to ask him Mummy?

He arrived just after eleven. The lady with him was his aunt, she said, and she had some errands to run, but would collect him promptly at 4 pm. Annette said that was lovely.

The two boys explored the rooms while she prepared a simple lunch of salad and egg sandwiches. They picnicked in the garden and then wandered down to the loch shore.

They were of a similar height but so very different in looks. Albert was almost fey. Wheatsheaf hair and such dark eyes. Duncan was happy. He chattered away to the quieter child about books and planes. About Daddy. About the school, and about things he would do when he grew. Like climb trees, he announced, pointing to the ones that bowed over the outhouses at the rear of the lodge. Oak and beech and small saplings -littered and thin at the base.

She followed at a safe distance. Weather could turn on a penny here, and she wanted to make sure they were safe. They skimmed stones and splashed, laughter rippled across the lawns that would soon host guests and she smiled at her worries and wished them farewell.

Although the baseboard for the train set was awkward to carry down the stairs, the three of them managed to get it safely into Duncan's room. Several more journeys and the tracks, landscape, buildings and trains were set out. Albert listened gravely as Duncan told him about their train journeys, first to Newcastle and then here, and that the man on the train who had given him American chocolate was staying with them until he found somewhere else. When he woke up and met Albert, perhaps he would give him some too?

After lunch the boys became restless, the Hornby train set discarded for the moment, and Duncan said he wanted to go into those buildings at the end of the back garden. There were three or four bricked closely together. Slates on the roofs slipping and gaps in the walls where the windows had once been. Frost cracked, she supposed. The sun warmed his legs, and his thoughts of getting his summer shorts muddy and his mummy having to wash them when she had so much to do to Daddy's house, vanished. Today he was exploring the outhouses with his friend. Three doors into separate buildings and a stable at the end.

He would love to have a pony. And a trap. Even though he would prefer a monkey or a dog. He had whispered the word puppy to Mummy on the train, at the picnic in Jesmond Park, on the nights when the air armada had columned above their Anderson shelter and she had pushed her hands against her ears so hard it made her wrists ache.

Or a parrot, he said to Albert. Brightly coloured – that could talk. Like pirates owned. Considering the names he would give his pets and what they would eat and how much he would love them, he pushed open the door to the largest outhouse and drew Albert in with him.

It was squat with a sloping ceiling, and smelled of coal and things unnamed; a tang and an edge beneath it. Were there rats? Standing in the doorway she watched the boys clamber over a mound, a light from a small window casting long light across the room.

"Be careful," she said. Rats and years of things untouched may harm them. Cobwebs and years of stained rust peppered the small window.

Coal and wood formed hills that they clambered over and around. Duncan wanted to reach the end of the room. Explorers never gave up once they had started an expedition. Even if they got stuck in the ice or perished in the Arctic. Like Edmonson. And Shackleton. Brave men. Like Daddy. Who never gave up?

Even if it was very cold.

Like Scotland.

It wasn't a big room really. Not like his new bedroom. He was thrilled with the train set that Mummy had found at the top of the house. They had had a lovely time setting it up. Quite a lot of it would need to be oiled so that the trains would run smoothly on the tracks, but Mummy said they could do that later on in the day.

"Be careful you two," she called from the edge of the room as they scrambled across the coal waste towards another door in the furthest corner. It was chilly so far away from the door and he bent to pull his socks up. Albert hung back. Curious yet worried. In the light from the door where his mother's shadow fell, he could see the white gold of his friend's hair like a beacon across these arctic wastes.

They had a cellar in their old home. You got to it through the door in the kitchen. It was very dark down there and freezing in winter. Mummy and Daddy had said it wasn't a good idea to explore it. So he hadn't. It had been used for coal. Poured through a little hatch that you could see at street level. Near their front step.

"Look," he called over his shoulder, pointing at small tracks in the coal dust leading towards the wall and he followed them with his fingers, padding behind them. They were small, clawy tracks. Sharp and clear even in this pale light. He bet they were mice. Albert didn't look happy at the thought of mice. Or rats. But Duncan said they weren't brave animals and would hide away from two explorers.

Red Indians were good trackers, he knew. He had a boy's annual – *Hotspur's Book for Boys* – and it had lots of adventures in it. He loved to look through the pictures and be like the boys in there.

The tracks came to an abrupt halt at the wall, against which leaned a long piece of wood. Rectangular in shape and looked a bit like a door, but it couldn't be, because there was no handle. A draught blew around the edge and he guessed there was a gap in the bricks that was causing this. It was too heavy for him to move though. And he might get splinters.

Which would hurt until Mummy pulled them out with tweezers.

Peering more closely he saw there was enough of a gap to squeeze through without ripping his jumper or shorts. His socks had collapsed around his ankles and the coolness of the interior nipped his knees. That was when she called to them and said Albert's aunty would be here any minute and she must put the kettle on.

Albert's aunty thanked them, declining the offer of a warm drink, and said they must invite Duncan over very soon. Waving them down the drive Mummy said a bath would be a good idea to get the coal dust off his knees.

XI

A man out of time

Often he would dream. Not always as he slept. Of youth. Of halcyon days, of his clever clocks and wondrous toys. Aristocracy, merchants, guildsmen, children would visit from his homeland of Austria and beyond. Admiration for his skill and commissions poured in, for his genius was not just in the craft of the making but in the design, the concept. Functional works of art that delighted the world around him.

When he was young, in his first world, his Lord rode to war clad in steel, wielding sword and spear. Now, in this world, lords did not ride to war. They sat in leather chairs as others marched in their stead or screamed through the air on silver wings. The sword had become the revolver, the machine gun, and the assault rifle. Catapults became cannons and missiles.

In the bunker, the role he played in the delivery of carnage had been small. One mercifully cut short as the Russians and the Americans tightened their noose, and the skies of Hiroshima and Nagasaki birthed the angels of death in a nuclear flash that sullied the earth for any generations that may follow.

New wars would be designed on the drawing board and in the science laboratories. Weapons to end all weapons and the world would burn. He did not want to be that man. Yes, he would hide away. But just as Hitler had found him, he knew that the others yet to come would too.

Unless.

He was a man out of time. For centuries. This was not his world and this world did not need him. What would his legacy to Lochnagar be described as? Monstrous, a macabre perversion of a Mary Shelley novel? His constructs would not be admired nor wondered at. None would talk of the genius in their crafting, design, and concept. Their remarkable alchemy. His birthings.

The day he had taken the book from the bunker, the day that he fled; those initial steps on the path to his own chosen demise, little did he know how twisted that path would become.

At first he killed for survival amidst the ruins of Berlin. The other victims would be a means to his ending, cold and calculating. Like the order in which one sets cogs into the shell of a clock, one before another until the mechanism is complete. With each death, contagion seeped further inside him, eroding the final layers of the man he had been.

He was indeed a man out of time.

XII

Ring of fire

The Blitz intensified. Night after night, and the incendiary bombs set the factories alight ,surrounding the Isle of Dogs with a ring of fire – you could feel the heat.

They had been to the theatre with two friends and were strolling along Whitehall when they heard the drone of planes, looked up, and there were dozens of them in rows and columns. Then the sirens went. It was all so unexpected. No one was really prepared..A warden insisted that they go into a shelter; Annette was loathe to, but realised the man was in a panic and so she said to Duncan it would be a bit of an adventure.

At six o'clock they were released; tired and fractious

Duncan wanted to be carried. The other Londoners they had shared the night with were agitated – would they find transport home? Annette was annoyed at them. Surely the events of last night would have urged them to be calm with each other? Especially as there were small children amongst them.

The driver and conductor of the 53 bus they finally boarded were as determined to get home to Plumstead Garage as she was to get to Shooters Hill.

When they arrived home, the daylight had gone behind a big black cloud and she could smell smoke and burning. All along the Old Kent Road there was evidence of bomb damage – piles of brick dust and rubbish, broken furniture and bedrooms exposed to sight. Looking back she believed that was the only time she was really frightened.

*

Albert's aunty dropped by unannounced that morning. She said she had made a few biscuits as a thank you. They sat in the kitchen with the fading paper and the sun streaming in. Duncan had decided he would play with his train set for a while, as Albert hadn't accompanied Dolly.

It was lovely to talk to someone, Annette said. It had been such an age since she had had the chance. Talking about the Blitz and the fear she had felt in the city somehow put things into more perspective. She hadn't liked to discuss such things with the Fosters. It hadn't seemed right. They had been talking for half an hour before the door swung open and the old man appeared.

*

He was dressed and was wearing his overcoat, despite the fact it was warm. Annette realised that she did not know his name, and so introduced Dolly to him merely as their guest. He bowed slightly and said he would go into the town to seek lodgings. He was grateful to her for her courtesy, and would return for his belongings some time later.

With that he left the room, and Annette hurried after him, opening the front door and suggesting he have lunch with them on his return. Thanking her, the old man walked down the drive and onto the road that led to the village.

Although there was a breeze, it was pleasant next to the loch and Duncan skimmed stones and dug furrows for the water to funnel into as the two women happily talked for what seemed hours about all manner of things. Annette learnt Dolly was widowed too, with a grown-up daughter who lived in Aberdeen and three small grandchildren. She missed them dreadfully but was hoping they would soon visit. She had worked in the factories in Hillington during the war years. Taking lodgings there for the week.

"We worked all the hours God sent, building the Merlins. Thousands of us. Proud to be helping the war effort."

Annette smiled with delight at this. "Oh do tell Duncan, he adores Lancasters and Spitfires!"

Above the mountains, hot clouds bumped against the peaks and began to roll towards the loch. Temperatures were so temperamental here, Annette said. Dolly laughed. "Wait until winter!"

On returning to the house for lunch, Annette wondered how long the old man would be. If she made a warm meal it would be cold for his return, so she settled on a salad and some sandwiches. Dolly made her excuses, she needed to go and prepare the supper for her employer. The two women agreed to meet in the next few days so the boys could play again.

"We can share stories."

Feeling happy that she had made a friend, a lovely one, Annette prepared the lunch. Duncan helped her set the table and laid three places. He had chosen some of the crockery with the beautiful flowers. The afternoon wore on, Duncan played with his trains and she opened yet more rooms making a note of repairs that were needed, removing yet more dust covers over so many beautiful objects. As she took a pile of sheets through to the sink there was a knock at the front door; setting them down on the large sideboard in the hallway, she went to open it.

Her greeting to the old man died upon her lips as she saw who it was.

He sprawled in the doorway. Not looking like the military man he purported to be. His cap was off and there was a leer upon his lips that made her suddenly afraid. His eyes were glassy and the smell of alcohol was so strong it seemed to seep into the hallway. Duncan stood with his hand on the bannister newel, a frown on his face.

"Was passing. Going for a stroll. Thought I'd pop in for a cup of tea. Take you up on your offer."

Annette felt a blush heat her chest.

"Jolly good timing then, catching you in…" A cigarette hung from his fingers and he exhaled as he began walking towards the kitchen, stopping next to the sideboard where the dust sheets were and stubbed out the end of his cigarette in a small glass bowl before pushing open the kitchen door.

XIII

Outside

Morning rested upon the vast expanse of water as he made his way to the small town. Summer rose on either side, clamouring in trees and undergrowth. Brambles overhung the verge, catching at his coat. Moss wrapped around trunks, its green velveteen swarming the trees that burst with leaves and blossom.

As yet he had no names for the flowers and trees. He knew that leaves were naming tools but they were foreign to his tongue and so he lapsed into the languages of his pasts for knowledge.

Birke, Eiche, Holunder, Kiefer.

This far-flung outpost reminded him of Austria in

some respects. A village community set in the countryside, where most lived off the land in one form or another. The hills perhaps smaller, forests not quite as tall, but equal in beauty. It felt the same, smelt the same. Warm and clean, with that whisper of innocence. It felt like home. Was that why the book had chosen this location? Amongst the hills and stones of ancient peoples, his puzzle pieces waiting to be merged?

Sounds reached him from the streets that threaded the village. Music; gentle, rhythmic, pleasant. He felt the small construct shift in his coat pocket. A response perhaps. He brushed his fingertips over its smooth carapace, gently stilling the creature.

He began to walk towards the sound, realising he recognised the tune. One of the big bands, though their name escaped him. But it was pleasing to him; his dry lips split into a partial smile and he began to whistle.

The source of the sound soon presented itself. Ah – the great British public house, the beating heart of the Blitz defiance. His eyes washed over the contours of the building, its brickwork, the small windows with their warm, welcoming glow. The sound of music, of laughter. Of friends and neighbours, of a community at ease with itself, with one another, as they talked and laughed, drank together and ate, as music danced through the air with twirling tobacco smoke.

He stood outside. The significance was not lost on him. It was as it had always been. The outsider looking in. For all that he was, for all that he could do, could create, he could not share in the simple pleasures of companionship.

He could not just sit in the circle, to laugh, to share, to sing, to be at ease with others. In his heart he had always longed for it, but no matter how far he reached he could never quite grasp it.

And now, after Berlin... he knew it was beyond him. He was changed now. And he needed a name.

He needed a base. A place to collect his things, to prepare, to build, to feed, to rest. Sleeping in some abandoned barn or outhouse would not suffice. He needed facilities.

To build.

Somewhere there were the bones.

And hearts.

Of the others.

In a village of this size he doubted he would find an abandoned barn or building anyway, or at least not one in which he would remain undisturbed for long. He needed a room with decent storage or something suitable close by. Somewhere where things could remain hidden, undisturbed until he decided otherwise. Somewhere ideally at the edge of the village, rather than the centre.

His English had improved. After learning of his final destination he had acquired two Bibles, one written in German, the other in English and simply married the passages together until he had a basic grasp of the tongue. English seemed such a curious language to him. To know the words was one thing, to learn to use them in conversation was entirely another. There were colloquialisms and slang, some using one word to mean another purely on the basis that it rhymed. Different speech patterns and speeds depending on where in the isles they hailed from. So as he travelled the rails with curious fascination he listened, he learned and now he had reached his last destination, he was confident he could manage enough to get by.

Despite his histories he was wary of new places. Faces that would turn sharply as he passed, and judge. Children who would run behind him shouting, calling out odd names that he did not understand but the mockery was clear. He wished he could move peacefully here until the time came.

Such a perfect, perfect child.

Lochnagar Arms. There was neither breeze nor wind, so the sign hung clearly, salmon leaping and a mountain backing the words. Unlike them though, there was life within. It reached him yards from the door. An undercurrent of sound and smells. Smoke wafted out of the windows on the downstairs level.

Hesitating by the front door, voices were raised inside. What would his reception be if he stepped amongst them? An old man with an army greatcoat and long white hair beneath his hat. A stranger entering without permission.

His decision was made by a man who opened the door suddenly and greeted the Clockmaker as he moved past him and away down the road.

Stepping into the room he could barely see through the gloom of layers of smoke. As his eyes adjusted, the voices raised in ale and games settled until there was an unwelcome silence surrounding him.

Men were standing at the bar, glasses filled with dark ale. A few were seated at wooden tables, card games and cigarettes littering the surface. An open fire, unlit, sat in the recess of the stained wall. It spoke of poverty and desperation. Of an enclave where the beer would numb their memories of the ones who marched and never returned. Sons and grandsons. Daughters lost.

Eyes on him, there was a pause within the room that hung there like smoke. Removing his hat, his hair fell about his shoulders and there was an explosion of a laugh from behind him. Turning he saw a tall man with a moustache moving towards him. Hand extended he introduced himself and said, "You must be a visitor to these parts then?"

Conversation flared and the Clockmaker was led to the bar opening. "Let me buy you a pint?" Inclining his head he said he was looking for lodgings for the next few weeks.

"No lodgings around here I'm afraid. Stay and have a drink though." Uncomfortable in the heat and foreign stares, the Clockmaker thought it prudent to accept, listening to this small society of men whirl about him. He wanted to remove his coat that was making him sweat. Sticking to his shirt and back. But of course he was unable to. For the small construct within his pocket would become alarmed and begin.

And it was not yet time.

Perhaps this strange ale would cool him. It was a thick taste upon his tongue. Heavy with malt and hops. Whilst his benefactor talked with the man behind the bar, he looked more closely at the room and its occupants.

There were no women. And no younger men. Men in jackets, caps beside them on benches, were drinking, talking loudly in an accent he found hard to decipher. He had attempted to remove all inflections of his pasts from his language but often he would slip and thus contented himself with listening to the man beside him who seemed to have no need for a response. He was by far the oldest he thought, but some of these men were late in their lives. Weathered faces from time in fields and boats. He picked up fragments of conversations. The price of hay and feed. Soaring costs of cattle at market and rationing biting deep into their livelihood. Farming talk. As alien to his understanding as he doubtless was to them.

The group of men deep in discussion over their ale abruptly turned around, catching his eavesdropping and he attempted a smile.

For a moment he thought they might invite him to join them, but the moment passed as they held his gaze and all he read in the faces was disdain and something deeper.

He found another glass of ale beside him, the barman smiling in an odd way at him. The man with the moustache had disappeared and he was alone within this room. A subtle change had taken place. The friendliness of these villagers had dissipated and he realised that instead of a welcome, he was facing something alien. The beer had made him sluggish and he knew he needed to leave. Several men had stood away from their games and benches and were approaching him across the square room, joined by the farmers who had abandoned their talk of livestock.

Gone were his preconceptions of friendly villagers. Instead he was hemmed in by anger.

A tall, heavyset man with the florid features of ale suddenly spoke. "Get out. We don't want your kind here. Foreigners. Go back to where you came from."

Shouts of "Aye Big Hen" echoed in approval as they jostled towards him, chair legs scraping back and more men stood.

He felt their anger like a palpable wound and within his pocket the small construct sensed its creator's emotions and began to stir. He couldn't explain that he was a survivor. Like them. He couldn't find the words within this foreign language to ask for acceptance and safety. He couldn't. And so bowing his head he moved in defeat amongst thick bodies and the smell of days that clung to their clothes. Past the cards littered in endless unfinished games, and cigarettes still burning on tables that would never welcome him.

A path had opened for him but the men kept close. A pressure of shoulders and hot breath upon him as they nudged him slowly towards the door. His hand shook as he turned the handle and the daylight hit him like a sharp reminder of a life he would never have. Soulless and abandoned.

Seated on a solitary bench outside the public house was the man with the moustache who had bought him the drink. Confused by the animosity within the room and befuddled by the strong ale, the Clockmaker stared for a moment as the man broke into a broad smile.

"No hard feelings I hope here? It's just we've had enough of the Polacks and the ITIES. Time to get Britain back to the British you see. I suggest you move on and find somewhere else to lodge. How does that sound old fellow?" He lifted a cigarette to his lips and inhaled, blowing it into a stream of air that whisked it away before the old man could respond.

"Right. Well that's that then. Best be on your way." The man on the bench remained still, his eyes filled with malice as he watched the Clockmaker slowly walk away.

Within his pocket the construct leapt to life. Scratching at the lining of the coat, frantic. He moved swiftly now, past the shops and the pond to a track he knew would take him to the final place. Up a small incline that left him breathless amongst copses of summer trees with sun that spliced the leaves and daffodils still blooming after the spring.

Finding an opening amongst the beech and oak, he sank to his knees and drew the small creature from his pocket. Its noises were piercing and anxious and he stroked and murmured softly to it until it calmed and lay still in the palm of his hand.

He would return in time, later, as the sun sank below the loch, to the house of the perfect one. Explain the lack of immediate lodgings and perhaps ask the lady to extend his stay. So much hung in the balance now. Constructs baying for their birth. Awaiting the call of the dolmans. And his soul. Encased and trapped within the blue aura of the dybbuk in the rosewood box.

All was energy.

Calmed, the construct slept a while as the Clockmaker, a man in search of a name, made his way across the fields to where the ancient stones stood erect. Whiter than the natural geology of the hills, they reminded him of scrimshaws. Scrollwork and carvings in bone or ivory by whalers he had travelled with many years before the Führer. Across vast oceans of fish and snow – to the Galapagos volcanoes. Such energy and youth. There was a time when he found such wonders beautiful.

Those men. Forever aboard tossing vessels, had introduced him to the splendour of bones and teeth, of sperm whales, and the tusks of walruses. Elaborate engravings in the form of pictures and lettering on the surface pigmented with candle black, soot and tobacco juice. He never recalled their faces.

Standing in a rough circle, the stones that the Celts, Druids, ancient purveyors of magic and science, had built. A cruciform structure of thirteen stones, seven beyond and five within. A place appointed for worship, where the chieftain would stand strong by the central stone, addressing the people. Robes and murmurs. Mistletoe and mystery.

Segments of rock lay in their midst toppled by a colossal upheaval. Whilst at the farthest end, where the hill sloped steeply down into another valley, there sat the table. Tilted, white, towards the horizon. An altar to some vast and primordial god that this country had forgotten. Or neglected.

Until now.

He ran his hands over their surfaces, reading the braille of histories; sensing their language. All was foreign here. There were other groupings on the islands far off the coast

89

of this cold country, but this dolman cluster was the one that would be the final resting place. For his soulless life, and the ultimate sacrifice. All his lives' journeys had been pre-ordained by something far greater than any mortal mind could dissemble. Each step towards this moment brought sufferings that he had overcome. Eventually.

He was so tired now. So terribly, terribly tired. The magical aspects within him fading rapidly as his time drew near. Creating his constructs as bearers, his legion of bone, valiant and strong and un-questioning; they would be his guides to the afterlife.

Two long rows of stones ran parallel to each other forming a serpentine avenue leading to the sunken, chambered tomb. A raised circular mound surrounding the chamber was pitted with fallen blocks, and he stepped upon it looking downwards into the pit. Within his pocket the smallest of his creations awoke. Gently, he coaxed it from its nest and placed it within the grass circle.

Hesitating, the construct moved its limbs, turning cogs and wire and bone in a gentle dance. Making no sound besides the movements within the carapace, it urged itself forward. Following it, the Clockmaker peered over the edge. Deeper than he expected, the sides were sheer, hewn from metamorphic granite by dead hands. Neither clay nor wicker securing its sides.

The light was dimming and the base of the pit could hardly be glimpsed. But it was deep enough for his deeds, and the rocks that lay scattered would be grave soil – sprinkled and concealing. The shuddering of soil. Can you hear it?

He wondered briefly if one ever glimpsed the Northern Lights this far north? What would they look like against these bleak and bleached remnants of a time when man worshipped things hidden and mysterious? Aurora Borealis. His final colours.

Tursachan Chalanais.

As had always been his intention, he returned to Loch House. Making himself bow-backed he re-arranged his face into one that was weary, trudging up the path to knock tentatively on the door. She was a gentle soul with not much worldliness about her. Playing to her good nature would be his way in to the family group. A gentle old man, more like an uncle, who would shower attention on the fatherless boy. A soft smile curled within him and he began to think of the many ways he would ingratiate himself over the coming weeks.

XIV

Till death do us part

"I apologise Major, but as I said last time, we are not open, and we have so many things we need to do, my son and I. I am afraid you will have to wait for an invitation before you visit us again. I would ask that you now leave this house."

Breathless from such a forward response to his intrusion, she felt her resolve waver as he turned to face her, his eyes hardened and the leer left his lips. She found herself backing against the bannisters. Her eyes never left those of her child whose tears threatened and she felt his shame. Trapped in their own home by this awful man who had breached the boundaries. For a second their house became a stranger and the cold that accompanies fear surged through her.

He took no notice of Duncan as his eyes moved slowly across her body, deliberate and unfaltering. Her rage had fled and she felt naked, ashamed. After all her grief, her longing for Gordon, the nights when she wept soundlessly in a room next to her child. All that. And now this.

"Come now," he murmured, so close she could smell his cologne and the oil in his hair.

"I am sure this house needs a man?"

There was nothing in her life experience to teach her how to deal with this. She had married young. At nineteen. Meeting Gordon, whom she had considered out of her league, at a local dance hall that her friend Betty had persuaded her to go to.

"You'll enjoy it," she had said to Annette, who was so shy she spent most of the evening backed against the wall desperately wanting to go home to her parents and a night of the radio and the big bands. Gordon had spotted her, he said, alone and frightened, and had approached her across the room. He said her hair had caught his eyes. A glorious thick auburn that he had wanted to touch the moment he held her in his arms in that first dance. It had been a gentle and courteous courtship.

Spending days walking besides the Thames, strolls through parks and along the Embankment. They would often go to the cinema, and occasionally, if money permitted they would have a meal. He asked her to marry him one late midsummer's evening, when the trees were still and the air was heady with late blossom and the scents of gardenia.

She knew that she would say yes. He was a gentleman. A kind, gentle and sometimes awkwardly shy man, with a wonderful smile and a humbleness that made her feel proud to be at his side. Their lives before they met seemed not to matter.

Till death do us part.

She had worn a simple blue velvet dress with matching hat that her friend had made for her and Gordon had worn his Sunday suit. The single photograph of them at the church door as husband and wife sat on the small table beside her bed.

"I promise to be true to you in good times and in bad, in sickness and in health. I will love you and honour you all the days of my life."

They had honeymooned in Rhyl. Staying in a sweet bed and breakfast with a view of the pier and the sea. It had been idyllic. Just the two of them. Long walks and nights spent dreaming of what was to come. Whispers and murmurs of a love that was so immense she doubted she had lived before him.

Their tiny boy was born within the year. They named him Duncan after the cousin that Gordon had lost at the Somme. He was a quiet and placid child. Dark eyes that saw everything, hair the colour of the sun. Like his mother's, Gordon had said with pride. She stayed at home until he was ready to attend the local school, whilst Gordon worked at the local council offices. They didn't socialise much, content to be in the company of each other.

Till death do us part.

War had been rumbling in the distance for many months until September with rumours abounding until Germany invaded Poland, declaring war on France and the United Kingdom. Gordon had turned to her that night as the radio issued the sombre news and said, "My darling heart, you know what this means?" She nodded silently. Men were still numb from the First War; you saw the injured still, the shocked and the maimed every day on the city streets. Homeless and mute.

Awaking that night she found the place where he lay to be empty. Sitting in his favourite chair besides the fire, the heat from the coals was at odds with the warm autumn weather they had experienced. Only today they had taken their young son to the park to fly kites and feed the ducks. No leaves fell.

Yet.

She drew her arms around his neck and kissed him gently. He turned his head slightly and a small smile started to emerge.

"My love," he said.

And right then she knew, in that deeply instinctive way that she never quite understood, that their happiness was over. In a second, the words from the church ceremony flooded her-

Till death do us part.

*

It was more of a haze as the rain finely sluiced across the

breadth of the loch towards the house. First the air changed and you could feel the damp seep through your woollens before it reached you, as behind it, the tide of rain would soon buffer the monkey puzzles and pines.

She sensed all this from her small space at the foot of the stairs. A space breached by this man who seemed intent on ignoring her requests to leave their house. Nausea rose with her panic. As she felt the situation could get no worse, the door swung open, bringing with it the hawking cries of gulls flying inland.

He stood in the damp entry, startled as he saw the Major whose hand was on Annette's waist. A seemingly intimate moment that he had interrupted, until he saw the terror and panic pass across her face as she turned to look imploringly at him.

In broken English he murmured apologies that he had been away for so many hours, unable to find alternative lodgings. He said he had taken a walk. His sudden entrance broke the tense triangle. Annette pushed away from the Major and moved towards the old man.

"Then you must stay here, you must, longer if you wish." Inside her, the chaos and fear that she had experienced alone in the darkening hallway remained, but she wouldn't allow either man, nor her child to see such emotions.

Realising he had been spurned, the alcohol that had fuelled his intentions was replaced by cold anger. Pushing past them he left abruptly, not uttering a word to the three people who stared at him with ill-concealed repugnance. He would be back though. That old man he had mocked in the Lochnagar Arms would be shunned and sent packing.

Leaving this woman and her child alone again. Rage seethed within him, and embarrassment. Not an emotion he was used to. How dare that old man have the right to a room under that roof? How dare she reject him?

She was attractive in a sort of middle-class way. Widowed. Young child. Any woman worth her salt would see what an opportunity he presented. A man, warm nights in a large bed, a father for the sad little boy who seemed to have no intelligent conversation whatsoever.

Stumbling past fields trimmed by hedges and woven fences that stood darkly stark against the grain and the wheat in the gloaming, his anger intensified as he brooded on the rebuffal. He was in no mood to go home to sit in whiskied silence. The Lochnagar Arms would be full to the brim with thirsty men and he would join them. They were endlessly asking him about his war heroics and although he admitted to himself that he exaggerated one or two, he enjoyed their sycophancy. Poor sods. He would use them to his own ends. Stir them up.

XV

Comfort

Morning sunlight woke her. She had fallen asleep exhausted next to Duncan, who had cried himself to sleep. Her dress felt hot and tired and she needed a drink of water and a bath. The tub was old with rust stains on the claw feet but the water was hot, and she put a bath cube in it and watched the dissolving scent unfurl as it filled. The pipes made a noise. Creaking the floorboards and ceilings, but it was a comforting noise so she didn't really mind. There were two bathrooms on this floor. One in each wing of the house.

Duncan was tightly wrapped in his covers. She left the door ajar so she could hear him if he called to her. Today they would go for a walk. Fresh air would be good. They needed distraction from the horrid events of last night. Along the riverbank exploring hidden places that willows concealed. Water animals. Moles and frogs. Distant foxes and always the stags upon the hillsides.

Safe from the shooting parties for now.

Drying her hair she pulled it tightly back into a bun and pinned it. It aged her, made her cheekbones sharp and stern. Her eyes, as dark as her child's, seemed bigger these days, a greyness beneath them. She had lost weight since the summer days with the Fosters. Nothing to worry about, Dolly had told her. Anxiety and grief do this to you. A tonic of rosehips. And iron. Vegetables, she had said.

Duncan loved the water. Building dams, finding rocks and stones to pile on top of each other, dry stoning the gaps with gravel and sand from the edges heavy with rush and weed. They had bought wellingtons and water shoes for paddling. A net and a bucket. Stacked carefully in the hall next to the walking sticks with strange heads. Coats for when it got cooler. As it could swiftly here, Dolly had told her.

She asked the elderly man if he would like to join them. Smiling, he bowed his head and explained he had errands to run. She made them all sandwiches and filled a Thermos flask with tea. Would he be home for supper? He said most certainly and there settled upon them a sense of a union and bond. It lifted the heaviness of the night before.

Duncan ran ahead, darting between interesting things and collecting treasures in his pockets. It was far too early for conkers or acorns, but there were leaves and pebbles and bits of bark that would be proudly displayed on a shelf in his room. Lined up in a jumbled order that told their stories.

She had brought along a book of children's fables that she would read when he dozed on the picnic blanket after lunch, when their lazy day had stretched to the dusk and they wandered back happy and full of the air from the mountains.

Bird song and green things. Trees that rattled seeds in a low wind that blew down from the mountains that sat around the lodge like a bowl. Duncan smiled at the thought of them being porridge in a bowl. He liked porridge, but only with a bit of honey, not salt. Mummy had said the Scots like to put salt in their porridge and he had pulled his "nasty" face.

Sounds of water reached their ears and they followed it; he would play pooh sticks from a bridge. Streams and rivers needed bridges. Or make a dam. Yes. Like they did in the war.

XVI

Mechanism

He would indeed make sure he was back in time for a hot meal with the widow and her son. The perfect child. But he had needed to go out without drawing attention to himself. To find the building materials for the final ones. Sinew and gut. Bone. Wire thread and cogs he had in abundance. The finest clockmaker Austria's guilds had ever seen. He had admired the work of the Windmills – Joseph and Thomas of St Martin's le Grand in London.

He had visited there, oh so many centuries ago. Gazing with wonder at the perfection of lantern clocks, bracket clocks, long-case clocks and pocket watches. He was a different man then. His hair dark and gleaming, pulled back into a tail at his neck and a moustache that caught the eye of many a fair woman on the streets. Living in London for some months he took lodgings near the Windmill premises, visiting regularly, his fascination with the intricacies of the trade growing each time. It was there in that small workshop he met and befriended Thomas Tompion, who later gave him the gifts of the clockmakers' tools in friendship and patronage.

Secreted in the suitcase above the wardrobe in his room were those very tools. So fine and delicate. Calipers, pliers, rivets and saw. Folded up in the velvet cloth pouch that bore his initials in gold. Embroidered by a woman who had thought him kindly and a possible husband.

London had altered of course this time, away for so long he could no longer find the small shop down the lanes and alleys that were smog-ridden with soot and poverty. Vast tracts still showed the damage from the Blitz. But – always

"Tempus Rerum Imperator".
"Time is the commander of all things."

He stood once more within the silent stone circle and breathed. The air, clear and cool, carried the fragrance of farmland, earth, grass and livestock.

Yes this was the place, the place he needed and perhaps it needed him a little too. He sat on the stone slab that lay at the centre of the stones straddling the burial cairn, and slipped his brown rucksack off his shoulder. Opening it he took out a biscuit tin with a red tartan border framing an artistic impression of a hillside. Cheese sandwiches – generous slices of locally produced cheese held tight by thin slices of brown bread cut into precise triangles; he smiled at the precision of Annette's handiwork.

In truth he liked the woman. She was of a good heart, honest. Their combined circumstances had pushed her into the role of guesthouse host prematurely. Her lack of confidence and uncertainty on where the boundaries lay between guest and host suited him well. And she was the keeper of the most precious piece of his puzzle, the sacred part, the rarest of pieces that had taken a lifetime to find.

Yet found it he had, with the aid of the book. Taking the flask from his rucksack he poured himself a cup full of its steaming contents. He would give her that – Annette did know how to make a good cup of tea. So much better than the poor fare served in buffet car and café where rationing still took its toll.

He took a bite from one of the sandwiches, chewing slowly with the stolen teeth that shifted painfully. He was not quite used to the taste of British pickle. Perhaps he would learn to like the taste of it. Good food, from a good woman. Yes, he did indeed like Annette. In another life they may have been friends. Ah, another life. How many of those had he had; three, four more? Yes: in another life, they could have been friends. He would have liked that.

It was just a pity for her that she had met him in this one.

With both hands he reverently removed his precious package. The ancient book wrapped in brown paper was held in place by a cruciform of string, the colour of sun-bleached bone. It was getting heavier now. Each page revealing more, as the book's mass increased.

Placing it on the altar, he untied the knot and gently peeled back the wrappings. Brushing loving fingers across its rough surface he leafed through the pages until he found one devoid of the flowing sanguine script. Next he took out his other treasure – the rosewood box. Cupping it in the palm of his hand he ran his thumb along the lid seal. A sharp animal cry from the fields beyond briefly halted his movements.

"Not long now my friend," he said to the box as he placed it on the altar surface. As he did so the box began to quiver.

"So. One life-taker recognises another." He smiled, placing a steadying hand upon it until it stilled.

"Magic remains in this place still, although it is not always that happy occasion for children at parties." He shifted himself and sat cross-legged upon the stone slab, enjoying the rest of his meal. Watching another beautiful Highland sunset, he waited.

Long shadows cast by the tall, thin standing stones began to poke the base of the altar as the sun began to dip beneath the surface of the horizon. The final moments between day and night, between light and dark.

The Clockmaker swallowed the last remnants of tea; the beverage had long lost its warmth and like the air around him, felt chill and bitter. He heard the slow ticktack of small, sharpened claws returning to climb the altar leg. Six sharpened metatarsals gripped the ancient stone propelling the small creature upwards and it scuttled towards its master, the glossy enamel of its body stained orange in the fading rays.

Pausing next to him, it then moved towards the open book, squatting upon an open blank page. Tiny cogs whirred, gossamer wires pulled and the creature opened its jaw. Slowly, twin syringes pushed themselves through its open mouth and the warm blood of the sheep dripped onto eager ancient pages, each spreading drop hungrily absorbed without a trace. Cargo spent, it returned sluggishly towards the old man, climbing into his coat pocket and nestled as the Clockmaker patiently awaited the next steps of writings.

Dusk approached, the sun low on the horizon, a sleep-heavy orange closing another day. And now, before the house, there was a special place he needed to visit.

An old barn near the summit of the hill stood sentinel over the lodgings, not too distant from this place of ancient worship and solstice. His reconnaissance of the area was nearly complete. He was beginning to understand the area well as strategies grew in his mind. Places to lay low, places to hide things, places to attack from, then retreat if needed. Yes indeed, he was beginning to understand the village well, if he was a dog he would piss in every corner. The thought made him smile.

*

None had encountered one such as he, an outsider within their rural life. The farmers, labourers, strong men, but their world was narrow, small, dull, their learning limited to the seasons and land. Even the names of their streets and lanes showed dullness of mind... Church, Loch, Ewe, Market. Roads truncated by mountains or penfolds. Too disheartened to explore beyond the confines of their parish.

Their hostility, evident in the public house, and fuelled by ale would nonetheless be surface-deep and he would have to use his age to his advantage from now on. They had not laid a finger upon him, held back perhaps by ingrained respect for older folk. But the longer he stayed, the more their antipathy towards him would grow, gossip would burgeon and they eventually would seek him out. In their pack they would shout for him to come out of the lodge, to stop hiding behind a woman's skirts, to face them as a man and take his leave of their village.

He had witnessed centuries of violence and intolerance. Witch finders, self-proclaimed and brutal.

Ritual, all was ritual.

Three of these villagers though would suit his purpose. Men of medicine, of property, law – cut from a different strength of cloth. Men of logic and learning. Worthy adversaries. The policeman who had observed the anger of the men in the public house from his quiet seat in the corner, would he have stepped in had the situation changed? His confidence was formidable, experienced.

An ideal donor. One more. A definite physician. Despite the signs of illness that he may not realise had settled within him, the Clockmaker saw keen intelligence in the man's eyes. An acumen fit to decipher the complexities he would soon receive.

And the third and final? A lout. A boorish brute of a manual, brawn and bristle and vulgar strength. An ideal trinity.

*

It had seen little recent use. Sunlight bladed in through holes in the barn's roof and gaps where the slats had dislodged in the double doors. Bloated dust mites easily seen as they drifted lazily through the light. Old straw and chaff patch worked the floorboards that creaked beneath his footfall. Some had fallen victim to the open roof and were soft and rotten, fragments of wood clinging to heavy nails. Picking his way cautiously across the length of the building past animal pens, gallowed beams propped the arching roof, a makeshift ladder led to the hayloft. Mounting the stairs, he allowed himself a wry smile at the possibility it would collapse. True, he would fall with the agonies of breaking bones reminding him that healing would begin in a heartbeat. He no longer wanted that.

Tools hung along walls on hooks. Spades, forks, a scythe. Rust had crept across them but they looked solid enough. Sharpening stones, old and worn, had been set aside on a rough shelf beneath a crudely glazed window that afforded him a clear view of the rear of the lodging house. The grounds to the west still bore the lines of a kitchen garden, separated by a soil path that ended in the outhouses.

Another had been at this window. Not the farmer who failed to return to sharpen the tools, but one with a more disturbing reason. A rough circle had been wiped clean on the pane. An upturned crate was at its sill. Marks in the grime of the floor indicated that it had been recently dragged there, upper surface hastily cleaned.

His fingers touched an indent left in the lingering dirt, a glass or cup. Other circles patterned the crate's surface. Smaller, closer together as if paired, an object repeatedly lifted and replaced. At his feet he saw boot prints moulded into the chaff, heavy and ridged. Crouching he picked up something that caught his eye. A cigarette butt, one of several littered around the crate. He pocketed it, deciding to unravel the mystery that had presented itself. Taking a final glance around for items of use, he followed the footprints out of the door.

XVII

Smother

Night crept slowly upon Lochnagar that evening. With great stealth it smothered the sun, eager to begin its short reign over the small village. You could smell its purpose. Tendrils of thin fog quested their way down from the hills and began to probe their way through the village streets. Those abroad that night, returning from the pub, remarked as much. With alcohol-fuelled joviality they spoke of goblins and ghouls, of monsters hiding in the dark as they passed the unseen old man shuffling his way back home.

The thought made him smile. His mood too light. Not brought about by the fermentation of wheat or grape but the inner glow brought by achievement. His day's labour had been long and hard but he had created much. His fingers ached and his mind had tired, but his invention had been considerable. Soon he would be ready, very soon.

Nearing his lodgings, the streets far behind him emptied of sound as men disappeared indoors. Making his way up the drive of the lodge he halted at the sight of a shadow that passed in front of the large bay window, interrupting the light from the ground floor room. Tall, it moved unsteadily into the light of the porch. Lifting a hip flask to its lips, the shadow leant on the stone jamb and took a lungful of tobacco before flicking the glowing stub onto the gravel.

The Clockmaker paused. If he moved, his footsteps on the stones would alert the prowler; if he remained he would be noticed. Stepping onto the grass he made his way to a bed of shrubs that would conceal him.

The figure raised a hand as if to knock, but hesitated before landing the blow. Several moments passed until the knock became a dismissive wave. Turning, he staggered back down the path, passing his hidden observer.

As he opened the door, the smell of the evening's dinner greeted him and he hung up his coat and hat on the large coat stand at the base of the stairs. Not wanting to startle Annette or the child, he knocked gently on the half-open kitchen door.

XVIII

Dreams

A shining red engine hauls three oversized carriages of varnished wood up and over hills, perfect hemispheres, carpeted in lush monotone green, hurrying along tracks of mercury silver that stretch off over the perfect hills and far away. Small clouds of clean grey cotton rise from the stack of the speeding train and float away into a sky of pale crystal ocean blue.

A pair of Spitfires tip their wings as they meander lazily between the small grey clouds. A pilot sits in his gleaming cockpit. Medals gleam upon the breast of a flying jacket of pristine leather. A handsome face, high cheekboned, tanned, a pearly white smile flashes below a well barbered 'tash in movie-star fashion. This blue-blooded hero raises a gloved hand in a wave of greeting as the pair of warplanes passes on either side of a red sleigh pulled by eight flying reindeer. They salute winter's hero with a victory roll and carry on through the crystal blue.

Over the horizon the click-click-click gets louder. But wait, that's not right, Spitfires don't click. They glide and pirouette. The clicking becomes louder as the Spitfires gently unravel into wisps of smoke. Crystal blue fades to a grey memory, as the end of a small bed becomes the new horizon.

*

Groggy eyes blink and try to focus. Moonlight peeks through drawn curtains and pewters the room's contents. Wooden toys bathed in silver scatter the floor. Posters of VE day are clear to see together with drawings of the glory of war, portrayed by the hand of a child. Red, white and blue. A young boy's room. His.

Though the source of the clicking cannot easily be recognised.

Small legs clad in tartan nightwear swing down from the bed and feet fumble into slippers of well-worn brown weave. With a slight tremble of the leg, Duncan stands and rubs his eyes. He reaches down and pulls his dressing gown off the bed and shrugs himself into it. He takes a semi-conscious patrol of his room in search of the curious sound, eyes easily picking up familiar objects in the light of the moon.

Young ears hear keenly.. But wait, was there something else? Not merely the clicking, but a furtive scurrying.

Something inside him recoils and with a few quick strides, the little boy leaps onto his bed. Pulling his knees in close to his chest, a shiver weaves its way down his spine. His breath is fast, shallow gasps. His mouth opens to call on his mother, but something stops him. Curiosity? A memory of a brave father? The man of the house should not be afraid of the dark.

What is the worst this could be? It was not the war that took his daddy and so many more. It was not a volcanic eruption like Krakatoa, a story in his annual. What was it likely to be in a house locked tight and sleeping? Mice? Yes. In big old houses with hollow skirting boards.

Mice from the outhouse where they had left their scritchy-scratchy claw prints.

Mice drawn to the warmth and tidbits beneath his bed. Big boys wouldn't be afraid of a little mouse.

His breathing steadied at that revelation. He wouldn't fear the mouse; he would catch it. A pet. He wondered what he would name it. Light. Of course. He would go and switch his light on.

Determination steeled his limbs as he sprang from his sheets and took the two strides to the light switch. He stood by his door, the wool of his dressing gown brushed his cheek as he reached up to the switch. His door was ajar, yet the warm yellow glow of the landing light did not peek through the gap. Unusual. Mummy always left the light on at nighttime. Maybe she hadn't that night as the moon was so bright.

Yes, that must be it.

Then the sound again. Clickety-click, scratch scritch. It wasn't in his room, it was in the walls… He placed his ear to the wallpaper. He could hear them faintly, mice, more than one. How would he choose which one to be his pet? Turning back to his bedside cabinet, he took his glass of nighttime water, gulping the contents. And then he went back to the wall. On hands and knees he placed the glass to the surface and listened. *There.* Clicking and the sounds of movement. He could hear it clearer now. Two, maybe three of them.

Slowly moving along the floor he followed the progress of the mice behind the wall. He didn't notice his knees were cold or that his slippers had come off at some stage in the crawling. All he could think about was where would the mice come out? Would there be a small hole they had nibbled over the time the house had been empty? He hadn't seen one that he could remember, but then mice were very clever.

As he reached the part in the wall where the fireplace was, he realised he would have to take the glass off the wall and go around the hearthstone. He worried for a moment that he would lose the track they were taking, until something caught his eye by the fire grate. A glint in a moonbeam, not a glimpse of a mouse. No. This was shiny – metal shiny – brass or copper, but not the metal of his fire grate that was black like coal.

Duncan tried hard not to make a sound. He looked for the tails, the small paws, the little pointy nose, indistinct with their brown against the dark.

Quickly he followed the best he could around the wall of his fire grate. Open, no coals, not needed in this summer time. The noise had started to rise. Glass to ear he rose on his haunches, then to standing as the glass chased the sound. It was going up the chimney. Motes of soot fell as gingerly he bent down, craning his neck up into the fireplace and slowly turned his gaze upwards. It was so dark.

So dark. But the room so light.

With the back of his hand he wiped away a trickle of fallen soot, and saw small shapes crawling away into the chimney flue. Shadows the size of apples, clicking away up his chimney. Claws on brick, dislodging the soot of ages. Had they been raiding the larder for cheese? Now using the chimney to escape detection and leave the house? Clever mice.

Startled, he saw one clearly. It descended towards him. Pulling back, he sat on the floor and stared as the mouse slowly came down the flue to sit on the hearthstone. Perhaps they were building a nest. He would catch them. Tomorrow he would think of a way that didn't harm them. Not a mousetrap. That wouldn't be fair.

He returned to his bed, happy. The great white hunter would catch himself a mouse tomorrow, his head returning to cushioned goose feather as the Spitfires returned to a sky of crystal ocean blue.

*

The cooing of wood pigeons brought a smile to his waking. He did so enjoy their calls first thing in the morning.

There was something comforting, gentle about the sound. A sound that spoke of the countryside that existed beyond his window, of a green, natural world shared by countless animals and plants, in balance with one another, in harmony. The pleasure of his early moments enhanced by the faint smell of a cooking breakfast and the high-pitched questions of an energetic young boy and soft tones of an answering, loving mother.

He shifted himself to familiar comfort on the mattress, resting his head heavily into his pillow, hands behind his head, breathing deeply, closing his eyes. As the tranquil minutes moved him towards full awakening, the business of the day scratched at the door of his consciousness and slowly crept inside.

*

A full night had passed since he had visited the dolmans; the bloodied script embedded by now by the ancient powers within the altar stones and the blood offering of his construct.

If, as earlier writings suggested, the dolmans were indeed the place he was destined to visit, then further instructions should by now have appeared upon the blank vellum pages.

His heart began to quicken as curiosity and anticipation took root within him. Images of possibilities found fertile soil in his imaginations. Anticipation of answers welled up within him until he could resist no longer.

Lowering his legs onto the floor, he removed the large book from its cloth wrappings and placed it before him on the small armoire under the window. As the earlier pages turned, he found that the flowing red hand had indeed returned. The words, weak and faint but understandable. With bated breath he began to digest the new information presented to him in this elusive language.

The text completed, he considered what he had learned. The dolman circle with its altar would be "the church". The power held within would require incantations to liberate it, words and phrases from this book he would need to practice to get the necessary inflections just right.

An unblemished lamb is lain on the altar, around which are placed the four hearts. The first heart, that of the Mau, protector from poisonous serpents, and the bearer of nine lives. One of which shall be gifted to conductor of the ritual.

Next came that of the beast of burden Yuya, the carrier of the new soul. Then the heart of the scholar to give up its wisdom. The last heart was to give up the strength of the body, Khnum, in which it was once contained. The translation of this was less clear; it translated as Minotaur – the bull-man or man-bull. The identity of this individual he would have to ponder further.

The hearts would have to be stored until the anointed hour. This could prove to be difficult, though. He needed something watertight, airtight if possible, small, flexible so they could be easily concealed. Something like a water skin, or animal bladder, tied and sealed with wax perhaps?

Then of course there was the matter of the harvesting. He needed more deaths. But there was something else.

Something that bothered him. After the ritual, the words of power spoken, the book simply stopped. Surely there should be more, the afterwards. The aftermath. This disturbed him somewhat. Perhaps he would need more blood or perhaps the blood was too weak, perhaps he needed a richer source. His thoughts were interrupted by the sound of a young boy bounding up the staircase. Returning the book to its hiding place, he took up his dressing gown and decided it was time to breakfast.

With the unblemished lamb.

XIX

Fire

It was a brisk walk up the hill to the barn that overlooked his latest quarry. A stout walking stick, his trusty field glasses and a picnic with liquid refreshment helped the hours tick by. Not that he had been able to glimpse much that satisfied him. The fine-figured widow seemed to keep her curtains firmly closed at the beginning of the day, and then was busy about the chores. Indeed he had seen more of the young boy and the old lodger, but his interest was held as their daily lives passed before his eager lenses.

Then it was off to the Arms, for a few drams and tall tales. It simply wouldn't do if "the Major" didn't make an appearance of an evening. "The Major"! The title always made him smile. Never George or Mr Evelyn. If only they knew!

Local kindling and logs rested upon the scrunched-up pages of yesterday's news. A single long match was all that was needed to bathe the room in that familiar glow.

He did so indeed enjoy the closing hours of the day within cushioned comfort, current literature of choice upon his lap, whisky close to hand. A roaring blaze warmed the room nicely – not that it was needed at this time of year during the day, but the evenings were becoming autumnal and there was something comforting about a roaring fire. The housekeeper always knew how to set a good one.

A wide, heavy, oak mantle topped the arched fireplace, decorated with silver frames; images of friends and family, hunting parties and birthdays, Spitfires, his battleship and in pride of place, Winston with the troops. Horse brasses gleamed above them.

He shifted himself into his comfortable chair; high backed, studded ox-blood leather. A summer dressing gown, the colour of a quality port, hung loosely over freshly pressed pajamas of powder blue. Quilted slippers that matched his dressing gown, resting on a tartan footstool.

This drawing room was well appointed. Generous furniture, heavy bookshelves packed with tomes – history, mostly military, Napoleon, Caesar, and their ilk. There were others, some religious, some of local interest.

A recent acquisition was of a fine display cabinet that held his fledgling collection of Maling china. Over the past few months he had begun to nourish a growing interest in

China. Its culture, art, its history's leaders. Bringing him to his latest fascination – *The Art of War* by the legendary Sun Tzu. He was particularly fond of Chapter 13, which dealt with intelligence and espionage. Very apt reading considering gathering intelligence had been the order of his day.

As his eyes scanned the first few sentences of his book, his mind began to drift to visions of the swish of childbearing hips as they walked down the village lanes, a generous bosom sadly well hidden. His eyelids begin to fall and soon the dreams begin to find him.

*

Music gently filters into the joyful scene, the radiant widow looks up at him with lustful eyes as they lie together entwined as one in a meadow of tall grasses. A bright Scottish sun warms the skin of his naked back. Sweet thrush song is slowly hushed by a faint, slow tapping that gently increases its tempo. A tapping of a cane on dry floorboards. No, not a tapping… a clicking. A large insect crawls over the sole of his foot and then is lost amongst the grass, too fast for his eyes to capture it. He feels the soft, plump yielding skin beneath him begin to lose its softness as it becomes wrinkled and dry. Gazing down at the face beneath him, the halo of hair spread about the grass greys, turning white as old age claims it in mere seconds, rosy plump cheeks wither and shrink into hard angles of cheekbones. Ancient eyes of arctic blue glare up at him and peel back the layers of his soul. "Wake up,

George!" the thrush screams at him. "Retribution comes for you." The long shadow of a man in a brimmed hat flows out of the tall grass and the sun is stolen from him.

*

George Evelyn woke with a start, his arms flailing, and the half glass of port tumbling from his fingers. Realisation dawned. "Just a dream old boy. Pity. I was enjoying that one." Gathering the dressing gown around himself he stepped over the glass and spilled liquid that stained part of the carpet. Housekeeper's duty, that. "Off to bed I think, let's see if we can get back to where we left off shall we?"

The fire was low, the room now draped in shadow. Movement caught his eye as he reached to switch the hall light on – damn, this house was dark. A small shape disappeared beneath the display cabinet. Mice no doubt. Or a rat from one of those poorly maintained farms. He hadn't the energy to find out. Close the door. It wouldn't do much harm. Might even end up in the fire. For warmth. The thought made him smile. Like pouring salt on slugs and watching them slowly yellow and dissolve.

A sharp breeze found him. Strange… did the bloody woman leave a window open? She was a fool. Clumsy. He had barred her from touching the china. Priceless, he had told her. Irreplaceable. Unlike her.

Not a window but the door. Ajar and letting the night in. Despite the amount of alcohol he had consumed during the course of the evening, it was unlike him to neglect to lock up. Couldn't be too careful. Not with the amount of valuables he kept. Most round here knew about his collections, had invited a couple of chaps over when the latest piece arrived. The doctor chap. Stout fellow. Good drinking companion. Didn't wear it well the day after though.

Grasping his walking stick from the mahogany barrel next to the hat stand, feeling the weight of it, the carved and polished ram's horn at the tip a perfect cudgel. Raising it he stepped out into the cold night, late and silent. How many of them would there be? Brawny, dim witted, a group of them would certainly overpower him. Caution stopped him from calling out.

The scream of a fox far in the mountains startled him from his thoughts. The air had cleared his head but he was in no fit state to go looking for trouble. Closing the door behind him, he tried to turn the key. He had told that fool of a woman to oil it. Yet another thing he would have to speak to her about. Twisting it more forcibly, the key refused. Exasperated, weary and becoming increasingly angry he opened the door and pushed a finger into the jamb. Tried again. Couldn't fathom the cause. Too late. Too dark.

He would have to push something in front of the door. Heavy and solid. A deterrent at least. Would slow them down if they tried to re-enter. Bastards. As he reached to close the door once more he heard a rustle from the rosebed to the right of the door. Raising the stick, he called out a challenge.

"I've had enough of this. Show yourself. Clear off."

The hedgehog slowly left the leaves, making an

ungainly path across the step. Lowering the kebbie with a mixture of relief and amusement, he pushed the piece of furniture against the door, wedging it against the handle. *Should hold for the time being.*

Lighting a cigarette he left the hall light on, giving the impression the occupant was awake, and made his way up the stairs. Sleep came the moment his head touched the pillow.

XX

Cleanse

More dustsheets were ready to be washed. She took them through to the kitchen and placed them on the counter in the laundry room. It was cold in here. The heat from the kitchen range never seemed to reach this far. Too cold and damp to dry any washing. She would put the clotheshorse in front of the Aga at night. They would be aired in the morning. She did like ironing though. It was soothing. Often she did it at night when Duncan was asleep and she would put the wireless on and listen to the Light Programme.

Duncan wandered in, dusty and blackened from playing in the outhouse, and she said he had better give her his clothes and have a wash down with a flannel. He showed her what he had found. It was a treasure, he said. Opening his fist he handed her an object. It was small and grey. And sharp.

Behind her she heard the guest cough politely, and she turned, his coat draped over his arm and a faint smile upon his face. She wondered how old he was. Not too old, for he stood erect and tall. A military man perhaps. He explained that he was going to go for a walk to the village and wondered if Duncan would like to accompany him as he could see that she was busy. Duncan bounced and said, "Oh, please!"

"Well, as long as you are good and don't stray from the path, then yes, of course. That is so kind of you…"

The man asked if she would like him to bring anything back from the shops. Reaching for her purse, she said she would be grateful and could she make a list. She had found a wicker basket in the larder and would that be useful?

"Yes," he had said and "Please, I do not want your money. Allow me to do this in gratitude for your kindness. It can be part of my rental as it were." His voice changed at times, an accent underlying the flat tones he usually used. An inflection, an undercurrent suggesting that perhaps English was not the language of his birth. A slight hesitation in sentences, as though he was searching for the right word.

She felt a blush spread and felt awkward, but it would be impolite to refuse. Handing over her list for eggs, vegetables, beef if there was any, and soap, besides a few other things, she smiled and said "Thank you."

Duncan changed into clean shorts and the cardigan that the Fosters had given him before Mummy and he had left for the train journey. Annette was knitting him a new jumper, a red one; with wool that Nora had given her. Knitting and listening to the radio in the evenings was something she had cherished, Gordon beside her, as the world spun away into horror and loss. Dizzy Gillespie, big bands and the BBC Light Programme.

Duncan took a stick from the wooden stand in the hallway, one with the head of a faun. Walking was a serious business and he was determined to be efficient. He offered another one to the man, but he shook his head and said "No, thank you."

She waved to them as they set off down the lane, until they turned a corner and the trees hid them from her sight. *How odd*, she thought, *this man is a stranger to us and yet he is not.*

Leaving the dustsheets soaking in the stone sink in the laundry, she used the tongs to swirl them gently to loosen the dust. She had made sure she put rubber gloves on as the soda burned and she didn't want to end up with chapped hands. So unsightly!

The clothesline was ready, propped up by sturdy wooden supports and the pegs ready in their basket. Gordon's mother had been so organised, self-contained. All they would need was right here, saving for the vegetable garden that they would plant as soon as she had time. Chickens would provide eggs. Noisy creatures but Duncan had vowed he would look after them and tend them. Lovely sunny eggs for breakfast. There was little she would need to purchase in order to make this house one for paying guests. Elbow grease, that was all, and she was young and strong and it gave her a purpose.

There was a wicker carpet beater hanging in the laundry room and she took it through to the main parlour to remove the dust from the sofas and armchairs. Her arms began to ache even though it was quite satisfying, and the dust settled in her hair and upon her clothes, but within the hour she had completed that task. Pushing the furniture to the edges of the room she rolled the carpet up to mop the tiles. The large French windows were open letting fresh air flow in, and she could smell the pines, tangy and medicinal.

Her hair had unravelled and was getting in her eyes. She pinned it impatiently into a tight bun. It was a beautiful auburn, Gordon had said. It was the first thing he had noticed about her when they met at the tea dance so very long ago. She had been on holiday in Brighton. He had been so handsome as he approached her and she so timid. She thought he would be proud of her. Her reflection in the mirror above the mantle looked tired. Gaunt, almost. The young woman who had loved a young man had disappeared through grief. Would she ever return, she wondered?

Fleeting movement passed behind her reflection, so quickly she couldn't make it out. Oh, they must have returned but how odd they had entered so silently. They would be in the kitchen then. Strange – the house felt silent. Duncan would always call her name even if he were merely in another room, checking to see where she was.

Smoothing her hair and her dress, she untied the apron, and walked down the hall into the kitchen. The room was empty. Puzzled, she called Duncan's name, listened for his reply.

Around her the dusty house settled. Empty rooms and so much to do. Perhaps the remoteness of this lodge was playing upon her mind after the unceasing noise of London. Shrugging, she pulled herself out of fanciful thoughts and poured herself a glass of water. She would have loved to make lemonade, but there were no lemons. Perhaps she would make an apple pie.

Outside the window the day was warming. She needed to think about lunch for Duncan and their guest. Pastry? She needed to use the eggs and butter before the weather turned them. A flan with an egg salad. That would do. She would sit down though to make it. Her feet were tired and the heat was making her ankles feel uncomfortable.

The table was broad and flat, occupying so much of the room. It surely had histories to tell in the gouges and marks. *Woodworm? Goodness – hope not!*

She needed a flan dish. There was one in the larder, she was sure. Passing the doorway of the laundry she noticed water pooling into the kitchen.

Her washing lay on the floor, water within the furrows of an uneven stone surface. Disbelief turned to annoyance at such an unkind act. Who would do such a thing?

Picking up the washing she placed it back in the sink and felt the anger tinged with unease. There had been tales of soldiers displaced and wandering the countryside. Poor souls, homeless, so damaged. Perhaps one of them had entered the house. Confused, lost.

Lie not nameless in the earth.

Her thoughts were interrupted by the sounds of laughter as the front door opened. Duncan ran into the kitchen clutching the basket, followed by the old man. Setting the basket down on the table he excitedly told her of their adventures. What the lady in the shop had said, the things that they could buy. "Chocolate, Mummy. He bought me chocolate. And there was a boy in the shop and he goes to my school and he was nice and the same age as me, Mummy. His name is Timmy. Can he come and have tea with us? With Albert?" He spoke so quickly and with such happiness that she buried her worries. The sheets, the pooling water, the furrows, the shadow. Too much flew within her head.

That evening, when she had settled Duncan, kissing his brow and allowing him to tuck the chocolate under his pillow, she asked the man from the train if she might have his opinion.

Cradling her cup between shaking hands, she told him the oddity of the washing upon the floor. His reaction startled her.

"Did you place it back?" he asked. And she replied she had, but pressed for reasons still.

"I shall search the house and grounds for you, but I suspect there is nothing to fear. No need to lock the doors, for perhaps it wasn't an outside agent that performed the mischief, but someone within."

"I am not sure what you are saying, but I do not believe in ghosts or things that haunt old houses."

He merely smiled and said that there were more things within the universe than they could comprehend.

XXI

Morning

He awoke with a filthy taste in his mouth and a crushing pain in his temples. The sheets were soaked with sweat and the room smelt of stale whisky and cigarettes. He had no recollection of dreams. Pity, because the one with the woman beneath him had been arousing.

Splashing water on his face did nothing to ease his hangover, nor did the sight of his face in the mirror. Used to be quite the catch with the women. Never married. That would have put paid to his affairs. Scant choice around these parts though. Apart from one. Nubile pickings.

Ah yes. Might pay another visit to the barn today; catch a glimpse of her before planning his next steps. Change his tactics so to speak. *Flowers and wooing? Worked in the past. Indeed it had.* Cheered by such thoughts, he ran a bath. Clean himself up. Shave, wax the moustache. Cologne.

Once dressed, he felt ready for the day ahead. The annoyance of last night had dissipated. He would make a call to the ironmongers this morning and get someone sent to check the locks. Doubtless the wind had blown it ajar. He allowed himself a small chuckle at the thought of anyone breaking in. The men around here respected him, some would even, mistakenly, have called him a friend. He'd pop in to the Arms and join them for a lunchtime drink or two.

Picking up his packet of cigarettes and the packet of matches he lit one. Marvellous that first drag, he must say. As he descended the stairs thinking about how his day would pan out, he was met by a scene of devastation. The glass panes from the open front door lay in shards upon the hall floor. The head of the walking stick was embedded in the splintered wooden frame, and from the mahogany hat stand he had dragged the previous night there hung a thick rope noose.

Images of rough fingers grasping his Maling china flooded his mind, rage smothering disbelief. Ignoring the damage and cruel joke of a noose by the front door, he stormed into the drawing room, pushing the door violently. How dare these peasant folk break into his home? His castle. By God when he found them he would deliver a serious thrashing. Reaching out he flicked the light switch. The cabinet was intact. The china safely on the shelves. A scan of the room showed no sign of an intruder. Puzzled, he hesitated. There seemed to be no correlation then between the front door being broken and his un-touched collection. The room seemed just as he recalled leaving it the night before. The stain on the carpet, drapes still firmly closed.

He couldn't remember crushing the port glass though. Waste of fine crystal. Damn it all to hell, he would have to postpone his plans for the day and set off to get the police. No good phoning the ruddy man, he always seemed to be out on his rounds.

Doing who knows what in this dull backwater!

As he turned to leave, a faint sound reached him. A ticking. Then another and another, increasing, strident, demanding. Hidden. Where was it coming from? It filled the room until as suddenly as it had started, it ceased, leaving a ringing in his ears and muffled silence. He knew that sound but from where? His mind scrambled to catch the wisps of smoke of a slumbered memory. Last night. The hallway. The closing of the door to lock the mouse in the room. Beneath the cabinet. Bending down he peered at the darkened corners. Saw it. Hiding. He'd get the poker and drive it out. As he reached for the metal object a muffled cough behind him made him turn abruptly.

The silhouette of a man in a long coat, hair trailing from beneath a brimmed hat stepped forwards.

"You," was all he could whisper through arid lips, as he felt something with too many legs begin to crawl up his trouser leg.

XXII

James

He had learnt the hard way that beneath the calm of the streets of an early morning, the Gorbals looked like any other working-class district in a vast city. Wide streets lined with flat-faced tenements. Pub on every corner and an undertaker's (open day and night) in almost every other block.

But the heaving population of Glasgow's immigrants, Catholics, Jews, Irish, fomented into a seething melting pot of violence that not even the war could match. An air of calm covering a multitude of horrors. Thousands living eight to a room, thirty to a lavatory, forty to a tap.

Came to work on the railways and the Clyde docks,

they had. Came for higher wages, for fuller plates, for what they conceived to be a better way of life than was possible in starving Erin and the wasted Scottish Highlands.

And now here. Such a small village where little had changed in a century save for the wars that had robbed the lads. Here in the Lochnagar police station that was an afterthought tagged onto the house he had been given, two windows on either side of the door with a lamp above it, shaded with a blue cube.

The office was a modest affair commanded by a large wooden desk. A weighty piece of furniture fashioned in dark wood, stained and polished, though not too recently. A leather square set in its surface. It was well-used, generous drawers either side of the leg space, empty, lockable, he had no keys. A few pictures still hung on the walls, parting gifts from previous occupants, he imagined. Figures from Britain's history staring out at him, perhaps their purpose to remind the occupant of the chair of the duty demanded of him in the position he now held. A stern-faced Victoria and Albert with some of their children, the old King just after the speech he made as Britain went to war. Chamberlain and Churchill and his V for victory.

A few brighter squares on the wall that desperately needed a lick of paint, spoke of hangings now departed. He wondered what had once been there; more figures from history, loved ones, framed honours perhaps.

He sighed and considered making himself a cup of tea. Perhaps a rummage through the filing cabinet again. Not much in there really. Old yellowing sheets of paper stuffed into cardboard folders. Misdemeanours – the odd black eye when one or more of the villagers had had one too many in the local. The odd romantic dispute. Livestock rustling that usually ended up being someone's sheep had wandered into the wrong field or through a broken wall. Mischievous children. Some stolen farm machine fuel. Nothing much that wouldn't have been settled in Glasgow by the mere presence of a policeman or a clip around an ear.

Perhaps he would get some fresh air, a turn around the village on his bicycle. As he made his way out of his office the phone on the front desk rang. That too was a rare occurrence.

"Lochnagar. Hendry here." His voice was drowned out as the sound of a sobbing, screaming woman assailed him. "What is it? Can you calm yourself? I can't understand you." He paused and let the lady at the end of the line compose herself. "It's the Major." Her voice was racked with fear and sorrow. "He's killed himself."

XXIII

Hanging

James Hendry had never visited this house before. There had been no call to before now. They had moved in different social circles. Odd that such divides existed in a village this small. What they knew of the Major was scant; a frequenter of the public house, a man of brashness by all accounts. Larger than life. A teller of tales. Not the type of man to be in the thick of the fighting, down in the dirt with the ugliness of war where the terrors walked.

One of the larger properties in the village. Hedge trimmed, lawns recently mowed, wide sweeping courtyard. There were no crowds of people about the house, just the doctor by the front porch of the building pulling heavily on a cigarette.

James nodded a greeting. The doctor offered a hand and a weak handshake. He was weary; eyes heavier, lids more heavily charcoaled than when they had last met.

"Suicide?" James asked. Better to get the business of the day over and done with. Neither man was in a frame of mind for chatter or small talk. The doctor took a deep lungful of tobacco and simply nodded.

"Afraid so," he exhaled. "Seen it far too often. Fighting men in the war," he sighed, "can't live with it, seen or done too much. For some the demons do not fade, until one day…?"

"Door locked?" he asked following the doctor inside the house.

"Housekeeper let herself in. Comes here three times a week."

"Touch anything?" The doctor shook his head in a mist of smoke. "Doubt she got a chance to, first thing she saw." He motioned to the body hanging from the bannister. The face was concealed from them, head drooping against the tightness of the noose rope that had ended his life.

Scanning the hallway he took in the expensive items that were displayed. China and silverware. Lavishly rich oil paintings of Highland views. What wealth was here, James mused. Amidst so much poverty beyond, so much wealth within.

"They're on their way," he said. "Coming over from Balmoral. Should be here within the hour." The two men would wait for the reinforcements. There was little the doctor could do until the body was lowered, but James said he would look around the rooms in the meantime to see if there were any indications as to the cause for this man's decision.

A scattered chair, discarded tumbler, a dried patch of liquid beside it. Lifting the glass to his nose he wondered if the man had laced his whisky with pills. Time would tell. Little else appeared to have been disturbed. The room echoed the hallway with its paintings and china, proudly displayed in an ornate dresser.

The man had travelled. Bringing back these items from the far ends of the globe. Japan, Egypt, China. Navy apparently. Odd to think he would have had time during the war years to disembark and make his way through the markets of such countries.

"Anything?" James turned to the doctor standing in the doorway.

"Not that I can see."

Their attention turned to the voices at the front door. Four constables entered the hallway.

It was a lengthy and unpleasant task that faced them, lowering the body of the Major to the floor, where it would be wrapped in a tarpaulin to be removed to the surgery. There was no dignity in death, James thought, the man had soiled himself and the smell of urine and faeces was overwhelming. Poor man. To have come to this.

Removing the noose revealed the harsh sawing cuts in the neck. Covering the face with a handkerchief, James motioned for the constables to take the body to the doctor's car. "Lay it on the back seat lads," he said. "We don't have a hearse or a Black Maria. It'll have to do."

As one of the men began to wrap the sheeting around the body, the Major's arm fell to one side. Stopping the constables, James took a pencil and peeled the pajama sleeve up. The wound was not deep, running across the wrist with edges of the incision that were blackened. Checking the other wrist, the policeman saw similar cuttings. James stood up. "Cut his wrists and then hung himself?"

"Looks that way. Careful how you move him lads." Reaching into his pockets for the car keys, the doctor left the hallway ahead of the men who carried the body down the steps to the vehicle. James watched them go and turned his attention back to the stairwell and the floor. It was the spotless sheen on the panelled floor that nudged him to a realisation.

"Gravity, James, gravity. Why is there no pool of blood on the floor?"

XXIV

Toast

At the end of the third year of the war, the curate of St Peter's suggested they hold a midnight service to welcome in this New Year. With bated breath they waited for the alarms and sirens. None came. As midnight drew near and the city was peaceful, she remembered her child looking up at the statue of Our Lord; a small, bright smile lit his lips.

Six months later the flying bombs obliterated that lovely church. Those same cruel wonder weapons would eventually claim her love in the final days of the war.

*

Annette hurriedly cut a slice of buttered toast into soldiers as she heard her son bound down the stairs. She had her hair tied back and wore her pale blue housecoat. She quickly placed the plate beside a boiled egg that stood to attention in a plain wooden eggcup. Duncan appeared at the kitchen doorway, a large smile as he spied his hot breakfast. "Morning Mummy."

"Good morning my love, did you sleep well?" She ruffled his auburn mop and placed a gentle kiss on his nose. Taking up a butter knife, he began to saw through the egg ready to accommodate buttered soldiers. "I didn't sleep well."

"You didn't? Why not?" came his mother's reply, her back to him as she prepared the tea.

"There were mice in my room and they kept me awake," he began.

"Mice? They wouldn't be brave enough to come into your room. They would be far too scared of the warrior in the bed!" Solemnly he dipped his toast into the yolk.

"But they did... I heard them... they kept me awake."

"Oh Duncan, they are a lot more scared of you than you are of them." She thought it odd that a child who loved animals should now be saying this.

"Mummy? Could you put a trap in my room, in the fireplace?"

"Oh Duncan..."

"Please Mummy?"

She sat down at the table with him, cup cradled between her hands and looked questioningly at her child who had started on the second egg. Turning the empty shell upside down as he always did. He was concentrating on removing the top of the shell.

"Have you heard them before?"

He screwed up his nose and thought for a moment before shaking his head.

"I think so, but I'm not sure. I've been having not nice dreams though Mummy."

Rinsing the cups a while later, as he wandered off to play in the outhouses, she thought again how curious it was that he should be afraid of something so small. He wanted a puppy, and sometimes a pony, but it was mainly the dog he had his heart set on. A collie. He had explained in great detail that they were the cleverest of all the breeds, and would be very useful in herding the sheep he thought they should have.

She smiled at the thought of a dog herding flocks of sheep across lawns that would at some stage be manicured and perfect for afternoon teas.

Oh really, she thought, what harm could it do if it put her child's mind at rest? She would pop down to the stores with him and buy a couple of mousetraps.

XXV

Ben Macdui

Pealing bells beckoned across the waters of the loch that lapped against the shale and pebbled shore. So peaceful a sound. One that would lull you to sleep when it was in a gentle frame of mind, or rattle your senses when angry.

Morning geese flew low across the shadows spilling from corries and Ben Macdui on the edge of the plateau. She had read that Ben Macdui was the home of Am Fear, "big grey man of Ben Macdui". Goodness. She so enjoyed legends.

They really must make an effort to climb and discover, *she thought.*

They would have half an hour to get to the kirk. Duncan was ready, smart in his shorts and jacket, socks pulled up to the knee. He had chosen tartan ones today, because he said he was Scottish now and must look the part. Had he brushed his teeth? He had, Mummy, and washed behind his ears.

Smiling, she pinned her hat. It was a beautiful pin, one she had been given by her grandmother as a wedding present, simple and frail, with a single pearl on one end. Checking her lipstick wasn't patchy she averted her eyes from the reflection of a pale widow.

They took a gentle stroll across the stone bridge, under canopied trees that created a tunnel of their own. They stopped for a moment so Duncan could look for fish. A couple of tiddlers swam downstream, but the big fish must be resting, Mummy, because it's the Sabbath.

Where had he heard that word she asked? School.

Ah. I see.

It was a simple chapel. Whitewashed walls and a bell tower, arched windows absent of the stained glass she associated with prayer. She had loved the church they had attended before they left for this long life journey northwards. Loved the light and lofty ceilings, the pictures in glass that spilled their colours onto the wooden floor. There she had found a sometimes elusive peace in the months following the telegram. Stained glass window, mural, mosaic, the colours and designs of table frontals and tassels, tapestry, organ case, carving of Christ.

Sunshine warmed their backs. A light breeze blew in from the waters. People filed into the building as the pastor shook each and every one's hand. As Annette and Duncan mounted the steps he took her hand and welcomed them to the congregation. How were they settling in? Don't hesitate if there was anything he could do for them.

She would not look at the headstones that pierced the lawns leading up to the church. Blocked her thoughts about her man who had never made that final journey home. No sacred ground. No flower upon a coffin. No service of remembrance held for her love. He would always lie somewhere so far away from her. Alone. She did not glance.

So terribly alone.

Inside, the church was cool. High ceiling, no beams. The windows were slightly open and a faint smell of new-mown lawn drifted in, wrapped them.

Beneath their feet lay the named flagstones of parishioners who had lived in the village and the far-flung homesteads. Duncan counted them. Nine in all. Read their names and struggled with the lines that were faded by footfall.

Lie not nameless in this earth.

Heads turned to look at them as they settled themselves in an empty pew near the back. A few nodded and smiled and a young boy sitting with his family raised a hand in greeting to Duncan. Feeling her shyness overwhelm her at such unwanted attention, she clasped her son's hand more tightly. How odd that such a young boy could give her such strength. The organist swelled Widor's *Toccata* and she felt herself relax a little with the rising passion of the notes as the pastor and the choristers passed them.

Standing behind the pulpit, the pastor welcomed the

community to this service – on such a wonderful cloudless day. "Let us rise and give thanks by singing 'When I survey the wondrous cross on which the Prince of Glory died.'" Duncan joined in with energy, his voice merging with those of the others around him.

Highlands and islands.

During the sermon Annette found her attention wandering. From the simple altar, clothed in white and yellow, to the fresh sprays of flowers on either side. Field flowers. Hedgerows had given up their bounty. Perhaps she could add her name to the roster.

Duncan was avidly reading the prayers, following the psalms with whispers, occasionally plunging his hand into his pockets. She had no idea what treasures they contained and would not ask. He was happy.

There was no apse in this chapel. Simply the altar facing east, towards the sun and the dolman circle that Duncan and Albert had urged they visit.

Nave, chancel, acolytes, apse. Such ancient terms. Like Sabbath. Long centuries of simple relationships with a god who had selfishly taken her Gordon from them. What ever-loving parent would do such a thing?

Someone then quietly slipped into their pew, interrupting her thoughts. He was middle aged, salt and pepper beard. Smart in a Sunday suit. Hat in hand. He turned and smiled at them, and turned to the page in the *Book of Common Prayer*. He knelt.

The service was an hour long and she was proud of her boy for sitting so sensibly throughout. It was a long time for young children to have to concentrate, when she was sure all he wanted to do was run through the churchyard and back to their house to play.

Outside people congregated, chatting to familiar friends and family. Beneath one of the yew trees there was a bench encircling it. *What a lovely place to sit*, she thought. *Peaceful and quiet.* Perhaps one day when Duncan was at school she would do just that.

Duncan had spotted a couple of children from his class and he rushed over to talk to them. One was a small, dark-haired girl, hair in plaits and the other a sturdy lad with scabbed knees and a shock of red hair. They chattered excitedly as she hung back, too shy to go and introduce herself to the parents who stood close by. A voice nearby said "Good morning," and she turned to see that it was the man who had joined them in their pew.

"Welcome to Lochnagar," he said. "Let me introduce myself. James. James Hendry. Local constabulary." He smiled awkwardly at this and she laughed.

"Annette. And that young one there is my son. Duncan."

He asked how she was settling in and she told him what they had done thus far and what they both wanted for the lodge in the future. She found herself talking far more than usual which astonished her, shyness seemed to have been set aside.

Lie not nameless in this earth.

Dolly and Albert approached them, calling out greetings to both. James excused himself and set off down the path beneath the lychgate.

"Did you know," said Duncan, who had joined them,

"that churches only have two yew trees – because they are poisonous. If you plant them, cattle won't come into the churchyard."

She asked why on earth cattle would come into the grounds.

"For the grass," he replied and sped off down the lane with Albert in the direction of their house.

They had an early lunch of meatloaf and potatoes. Dolly complimented her on her cookery skills, which made Annette blush. She was a natural. Could she let her have the recipe? As Annette wrote it down the two boys announced they would like to climb the big hill and see the standing stones. Puzzled, Annette looked to Dolly for clarity.

"They're well worth a visit," she said. "It's a bit of a climb but you can sit down at the top." The boys listened excitedly as Dolly explained a bit about the standing stones. They were in a circle with a path running down the middle and a makeshift altar.

"Although I doubt anyone got up to any mischief up there all those thousands of years ago. So no horror stories for you two!"

Duncan turned imploringly to his mother. She hesitated before saying yes; if everyone was in agreement they could take a slow stroll to see them. It would be nice to get to know a bit more of the place that was now their home. But they would have to wait whilst she packed up some food and made a Thermos.

As they made their way through the village, Dolly

greeted people, introducing them to Annette and Duncan. It made Annette feel less like a foreigner here, with her southern accent and damaged life. Offers of afternoon tea were made and she arrived at the top of the mound where the stones stood with a light heart.

It was remarkably flat at the summit, bracken and moss and heather intermingled with grass. A large puddle in the centre of the grey standing stones had become a lake from the rain that had fallen sporadically during the last week, reflecting the sharp blue of the sky and fair weather clouds that paced their way above. The boys raced off, threading between the inner circles before dashing down the straight avenue of small stones to the edge of the plateau. Below them looped the loch, wrapping itself around one half of the mound, whilst behind them lay the village.

Grey and flat, some edges of the stones looked hewn, slanting towards the inner circle. She wondered what tales they could tell. Where had these stones come from in a landscape bare of rock? Had they been hauled here from far-off places? She doubted she would ever know. But there was peacefulness about this place with the clearness of the day around them and wheeling swallows dipping like bats towards the shores of the loch below.

Finding a suitable place, the women laid out the blanket and unpacked the picnic. Scones and some sandwiches, tinned plums and cherries. Two Thermos flasks of tea. As they watched the boys explore every section of the stones, Annette remarked that the dolmans looked like figures. Tall, grey figures. Keepers of this place for 4,000 years, Dolly believed. There was a splash and shriek of laughter.

150

Turning, they saw Duncan ankle-deep in the water. Albert glanced across at Dolly, waved and jumped in too. Their laughter echoed around the summit.

"I think we have a firm friendship there," smiled Annette, happy to see her child so content.

Before the boys joined them for the picnic, they took off their shoes and socks and laid them on a stone table in the midst of the dolmans at the edge of the water-filled hollow. The sun would dry them out, Duncan assured Albert.

As their day drew to its end, the shadows cast by the stones lengthened like needles compassing their direction towards the looming heights of the corries. Duncan asked if he could go to the farthest end of the circle where the tallest of the grey stones stood at the lip of a deep pit covered by slabs. Annette shook her head and said no, in case it was dangerous.

"We have no idea what could be in there, my love. One slip and you could hurt yourself." Disappointed, Duncan wandered off to collect the shoes and socks.

They made their way down the slope and into the village as the lights began to be lit in front rooms and a silence settled around them. Cloudbanks dragging night were edging their way over the mound throwing the standing stones into sharp focus against the sky. From where she stood, they looked larger than when they had been amongst them. A trick of the light, no doubt. How odd to be there for so very, very long, upright and tall. Proud sentinels over this valley, built by ancient hands for whatever purpose they had served.

They said their goodbyes at the entrance to the lane

where Dolly lived and made their way up the sharp rise to Loch House. A blue mist grazed the ferns along the road, hovering as if unsure of where it needed to go. In the dusk the house looked stern. Unwelcoming. And for a fleeting second, Annette thought she saw an expression of anger on the face of the house.

*

His mummy was busy so he decided he'd pop upstairs and get a couple of the Hornby trains. They needed a bit of a polish and perhaps some oil on the wheels. They'd made a slightly scratchy sound as they went round the tracks.

Reaching the top of the stairs he noticed the door to the old man's room stood open. Curious to see the usually closed room he paused to listen for a moment and then knocked. There was no answering reply as he craned his neck around the door.

An iron bed was well made, neat corners and a bed blanket of dark blue tartan draped across the foot of it. In the right-hand corner a heavy wardrobe with a long mirror reflected him standing in the doorway.

To his left a small desk with a view of the hill behind the house. It was a different view to his and Mummy's. The room was tidy, everything packed away. Grown-ups did that. He supposed in time he would be expected to keep his room this way too. *But not yet.*

The hill through the window looked much larger than he had thought and he wandered over to have a better look. The big barn that was out of bounds sat on it, how did people get to it? *Bit of a strange place to have a barn. All on its own with no animals.*

Leaning against the desk he pulled the curtains further open to get a better look. Which is when he saw a most curious object on the windowsill. He hadn't noticed it at first because the lacy bit of the curtain had hidden it. There were a lot of lacy curtains in the house and he wasn't sure he liked them. They needed a lot of washing and starching and Mummy was already busy enough as it was.

It was a cage of dull iron, secured to a white dinner plate by tiny silver screws. In the middle spun a small copper globe. Others with small armatures of golden wire circled it, dipping and weaving so slowly. It was like a lovely dance, he thought.

Around the cage rotated three cogs, gold, silver and brass. As they moved they shifted positions. Concentric to slowly crossing each other's axes. How they were held there was a complete mystery to the young boy, it was if they were suspended in air. Like the planets.

Resting on top of the cage was a small obsidian stone, edge faceted with many angles; it gave off tiny warmth against his fingers as he reached to touch it. Like gently cooling coal. From the top of the stone was a slender thread of wire upon which was a tin dial. Fine gold filigree hands adorned with strange swirling symbols ticked their way around the dial. It was so beautiful. Had Mummy found it up in the attics with the rest of his grandmother's things?

"Do you like it?"

Duncan jumped at the sound of the voice and began

to stammer an apology as a blush flooded his cheeks.

"It is beautiful yes… this clock?"Duncan nodded, embarrassment and guilt threatening to send him running out of the door.

"Before I came here I used to make clocks. Toys and clocks."

"You made this sir?"

"I did. Would you like a closer look?" As he did, the old man rested his hand on Duncan's shoulder and said,

"Can you keep a secret?"

XXVI

The Night Watchman

Leaning back in his chair, Craig "Hen" McGlennon let out a tired groan, swinging heavy boots to rest on the large wooden slab in front of him. It was a long night this, the air humid and stuffy. Smelling the carcasses that despite cold storage reached his nostrils. Ale would help. Sipping from his battered tin cup he scanned the pages of the local newspaper. Nothing much to report. Never really was. Good thing mind, made his life easier. Obituaries, sad them. Weddings – no one he knew. His missus might, mind you. Woman knew all hereabouts. Births. Small articles about cattle rustling, jobs on neighbouring farms. No roaming poachers who took a fancy to raiding the abattoir. Be daft to with him in here.

He knew many of these folk that were mentioned, from the village and outlying areas. Farm folk. Lived here all his life he had, couldn't imagine anywhere else he'd rather be after his war years, such horrors. The Arms most nights and then home to the wife.

She was a good 'un. Five kids and never missed a trick. Their oldest was nearly sixteen bless her, soon be ready to head off into service. Several chances around but he fancied the new lady over at Loch House might need help. Family would be here for a good while no doubt. Edney would be sound there.

He'd known the old lady from when he was a youngster. Played with her lad up by the loch and in the gardens at the back where the stables and the stream lived. There'd been a good few their age then. All went to school together, where his bairns did now. For a moment the years rolled away and he saw them, legs flying, loud and happy before the war came and led them away from here forever.

Not much to steal tonight here mind. Couple of carcasses hanging in the padlocked cold room. Next delivery in the morning, a few farmers who had sold livestock at a nearby market. Not good milkers, ideal for Hen and his meat trade. He heard the sounds from the Arms – a right old time it sounded like. Odd how sound travelled when you were on your own.

His fingers strayed to the key on the ring fixed to his belt for the outbuildings where the pens and corrals were. Tapped. Secure. Animals were herded in and then the lads would get to work. He'd helped out once or twice but truthfully? He didn't have the stomach for it. The noises and the screams were far too close to the noises of war.

Far too close.

A quiet life thus, and a night watchman's wage – not too bad. The war years had drained him, as it had the others in his regiment. He'd made lifelong friends though. Not with foreigners though. Never very keen on foreigners. The Welsh for one. And the Poles.

He recalled the old man with the soft accent who had wandered into the pub earlier that day. The Major made a right fool of him, thinking he could just walk into their pub and order a drink. They had seen him off though right sharpish. Good riddance. Had enough of foreigners.

Tricky bastards.

Newspaper discarded, he stretched again for the umpteenth time that night. Old wooden shelves lined with files and ledgers to his left and behind him the metal filing cabinet, stack of three broad drawers, navy. The walls a strange, pale green. Tiling in the carcass area made it easier to hose down. Sweeping in here took time, but it gave him something to do.

As he walked around the room, the candlelight flickered shadows, like imaginations of walking upon the sea floor. 'Fey', his grandmother would have called such thoughts.

Big heavy desk, worn and chipped, black telephone pinning stacked papers. A tin of sandwiches and a half-empty bottle of ale waited. A pair of wide drawers, one of which held his collection of Arthur Conan Doyle and his favourite detective. Odd reading for a night watchman, but then jobs were scarce after the war, weren't they?

Leaning gently against the drawers was "Basher", his old cricket bat. He reached down and lifted it onto his lap. Many an hour spent at the crease, days of glory in the heady times of youth. He ran his fingers over the three letters carved into the wood, the word bringing a smile to his lips. "Hen". After Hen Broon, the cartoon character, of noticeable height. Proud of that nickname he was.

His thoughts, which often returned to days when his life was so different, were interrupted as a shadow passed beyond the open window. Leaning forward, he swiftly reached for the bat and peered out into the black. So much for a quiet evening in! He wasn't in the mood for daft goings on. Tired and not a little fractious, the thought of having to deal with trespassers when he should be fast asleep annoyed him. Hadn't they anything better to do than ransack the outbuildings and break into the office in search of cash? Idiot lads.

Pushing the chair back he went over to the window. A fruitless act. All he saw was a sagging face reflected in the glass. Heavy bags and ruddy complexion, he looked tired and there were deep lines around his mouth. Where had he gone? Mebbe he'd nip outside and check the outbuildings. Bit of fresh air before settling till the day shift of the meat men.

The night beyond stretched in its endlessness. Must have been a cloud passing. He relaxed a little, a wee dram and a few pages of Sherlock then he would do his rounds, put his feet up and nap.

Reaching for the bottle, a high-pitched howl sung out in the night. His heart leapt into his mouth as he gripped Basher tightly. The cry came again. Shrill and echoing. Realisation dawned. Laughing to himself he shook his head. Nothing to worry about then – just that fat bastard cat. The mangy thing nearly scared him half to death. "Gas bottle". Damn thing was getting more rotund every day. Plenty of rodents and juicy titbits to be found round here. It was starting to resemble a damn gas bottle. They named it not for what it put into itself, more of what came out the other end. The thought made him smile. Another screech came, high and full of venom – catfight? It was followed by another cry, almost mournful.

Hen smiled as he filled his mug. The resident ginger tomcat come to see you? Ah Gassy, always the successful mouser. Be nice to have company in the wee hours, even if the company smelt to high heaven.

He sat down heavily, cup in hand, and opened the drawer. A few minutes to catch up on the goings-on in Baker Street. As he turned the pages the office door creaked slightly. High winds off the Cairngorms and moors. No wonder Gassy wanted in.

Turning in anticipation of the daft bugger, a sound within the small room distracted him, metallic clicking that jerked his head towards the filing cabinet. Just out of focus, something small scuttled behind it. Mouse, spider? Too small for a rat… looked more like a spider, bit damn big for a spider. Was the night playing tricks on his tired mind?

As he reached to switch on the table lamp, a fierce gust threw the door open, spilling dust and leaves onto the floor, crashing it against the wall. Such noise now filled the room as the filing cabinet jolted away from the wall, files spilling from the top. Thrusting himself to his feet, he grasped Basher firmly as another creature scuttled to the shadow of the skirting board and behind the desk. What on earth…?

Something was definitely behind there, a big one an' all. It was the smell of the meat. No matter how much he hosed the tiles or turned the cooling system higher, it was always there. A low, seeping smell that got into your head and stayed there hours after you left.

The door swung back on itself, shutting out the sounds of the night and the wind. Silence settled. Big Hen laughed. Rats. That's what it was. Hiding in the warmth. Attracted by the smell. That's what it was. Nothing more, nothing less. Lonnie would have to get the rat catchers in. Bad for business if the place was overrun.

Most probably rats hiding in the warmth. Might be useful to let that cat in after all.

Opening the door that led into the yard and the outbuildings, the darkness was dense and unending, stretching away to the sounds of the village and the barren hills that surrounded their town. It was too black, he thought. He couldn't see the shadows of the buildings or the trees. There was no edge to the hills he knew sat across the fields from this building – even the path before him was so dense as to have disappeared completely. Stepping outside he whistled for the cat, waiting for the familiar patter on the gravel and stones, as it would round some corner.

Craning his head to pick up the familiar mewlings, he heard instead a noise from the outbuildings. At the sound of his voice, the noise stopped abruptly.

"Ach," he thought. "I'll leave the door open for it. Too dark to venture out." Turning back into the room he thought it best if he trapped the rats himself. Them getting into the cold room would damage what meat was in there, and it would cost him dear if that happened.

His nerves were getting the better of him as the door pushed slowly open and the cat arrived.

"Bloody hell Gas Bottle. What kept you? Now get stuck in there and find that rat for me, will you!"

Ushering the cat towards the filing cabinet proved easy as the clickings and scurryings caught its attention. Scratching at the edge it began a low-pitched yowling that ricocheted off the walls. Frantic, it tried to get behind the unit as Hen raised the bat, his range measured, assured of the strike. The clicking increased, as did the howling of the cat.

Prodding the bat between the cabinet and the wall dislodged the rodent and it skittered away from him, knocking over the waste-paper bin. Papers scattered, there was a clang of glass as a forgotten empty bottle rolled across the floor and then he heard a second noise above him.

He gingerly stepped forward and made a hesitant pursuit. There, under a sheet of paper, a shape moved. The paper slowly began to move cross the floor, *click-click*. His raised his head just a split second too late. Behind him there was the sound of a footfall on the doorstep.

It landed on his back. Heavy, squirming. Sharp legs digging deeply into his shoulder blades as it scrambled, pierced, claws gaining purchase on his sweater. This was no rat. Clawing back over his shoulder, fingers stricken in panic as he felt it shift, avoiding his grasping. Scuttle and grip. His other arm reached up from the small of his back, straining, his thumb brushing something, no hair but smooth like porcelain.

Roaring in frustration and pain, he began to drag off his clothing. With his jumper half over his head he howled as it darted underneath his clothing and pinpricks in his flesh told the tell-tale sign that the thing had raced up his back and was sitting upon his neck. Ticking. Pricking. He felt the weight of it just below his hairline.

The pain as it dug its legs into the flesh of his neck, oh God, eight pinpricks of agony on either side of his spinal column. Freezing in terror he barely noticed the sound of the ratchet mechanism, as it peeled back its flap of stolen necrotic flesh revealing two hair-thin needles attached to pencil-thin syringes, filled with thick, viscous liquid the colour of tar.

A single scream faded within him as the needles pierced his flesh and the liquid hurtled into his spine. His face convulsed, left cheek cruelly twisting into the beginnings of rictus. A single tear leaked from his bulging eyes as they finally clouded.

It was within those last seconds he glimpsed the silhouette in the doorway, standing so still it may well have been a shadow. As it moved towards him he prayed deep within him that here was help – until he saw the long, white hair of the man he had taunted.

His body that had carried him well for so many years failed, and for a few moments he thought he felt euphoria before paralysis took hold, followed by the final falling curtain of oblivion.

"Thank you," the shadow whispered.

XXVII

Micelines

Their guest complimented her on the meal. He had two servings and said the dumplings were the finest he had ever tasted. Despite herself, she felt proud and went a bit pink and coy. It was nice he wasn't dining in his room tonight, and she felt she would enjoy sitting with her guests when they ate in the dining room. It felt for a moment like family.

Duncan was tired and asked if he could be excused. The river air and a full tummy, she said, and smiled at her beautiful child. She tucked him in and kissed his nose and told him she was so proud of him. His breathing softened and she watched as he slipped away.

*

The dreamer returned to the land of perfect hills and green monotone. Once again the Spitfires flew overhead, they looped the loop, performing victory rolls as they were joined by the Lancasters.

Below them the train did not run on the lines of shiny mercury. Tonight mice roamed the countryside. Giant creatures, brown of fur that sniffed the ground or sat back on their haunches and preened their whiskers. Smaller specimens sped around their feet, their fur a much duller lustre. Were they tin? Sprouting sharply out of their backs were small, slowly spinning keys of brass and steel. They sped off over the hills and far away as the clicking came. It got louder and louder and the mice stopped what they were doing and turned to stare at the dreamer.

*

The sound slowly roused him, pulling him upwards and awake. He opened his eyes but did not move. He kept his breathing shallow, eyes wide open, a mischievous smile born out of anticipation as the long seconds dragged. The clicking slowly made its way across his room. Seconds ticked with every click and scurry. Long minutes turned into eons for him, but he willed himself to lie quite, quite still.

Like a wooden soldier in a box.

Mummy said that patience was a virtue, and his was happily rewarded with a loud snap! Was that a tiny little whimper? There was a flurry of activity as many tiny feet scuttled and scratched up their escape flue, leaving their fallen comrade to his fate.

Duncan sat up. The moon was generous once more, bathing his room silver grey. He saw familiar objects scattered on his floor, just as he had left them. The locomotive silent at the station. One of the trees had fallen over but perhaps there was a strong wind in miniature land.

As usual his bedroom door was ajar and the wedge of yellow light painted the wall almost to his fire grate. He jumped out of bed and crept forward, eager to examine his pet. The trap had jumped out of the fire grate and lay upside down on the floor. It wasn't lying still. The mouse was still alive! Tiny little legs squirmed under the weight of the trap.

There were too many legs, this wasn't a mouse! The legs looked pale grey in the moonlight, ending in sharp points, insect-like. They writhed and jerked. It was horrid. He had so wanted a mouse, not this.

Duncan edged forward, childlike curiosity overcoming the cold stab of fear. With slightly shaking limbs and ragged breaths he propelled himself slowly nearer, and closer, his eyes never leaving the struggling creature.

He had reached cautiously for his fallen drumstick, gripping it tightly, poised to strike as the door behind him swung open. The landing light flooded the room as he turned and fell back onto his bottom. There stood in the doorway an adult-sized shadow. It filled the doorway, an object held tightly in a clenched left fist.

Startled, the boy inhaled deeply his mouth opened to cry out. The word shrivelled on his lips only to be released as a faint whisper of "Mummy" when the shadow flicked on the light.

His voice caught on his lips. He wanted his Mummy. He didn't care about the mouse thing in the trap anymore. Sitting there, surrounded by his room and all the wonderful things in it, he wanted his Mummy.

Until the light went on.

It was the old man, a heavy navy dressing gown tied at his waist over pajamas. He still wore heavy boot socks, though. The man smiled gently at the startled boy, raising a finger to his lips. "We don't want to wake your mother." Duncan nodded blankly, frozen, unsure how to react. Approaching the boy, he crouched down beside him and whispered,

"What have we here?"

"I thought it was a mouse... but it isn't," whispered Duncan, eyes round and deer-like, trapped between the hearth and the man.

"Shall we see?" He covertly pocketed the object he had been carrying and gently took the drumstick from the child.

"You don't need this, my dear. Ready?" the old man smiled.

Duncan nodded; it was fine. It wasn't a burglar or a ghost. It was the man. And that was fine.

After Mummy, this man was safe.

The Clockmaker levered the drumstick under the trap and with a flick of his wrist flipped it over. A sharp intake of breath escaped the child as his mind struggled to comprehend what he saw. Pinned by the steel bar across its abdomen was some kind of insect. It looked like a very, very big ladybird. But God hadn't made this had he? It appeared to be made entirely of bones.

"What is it? Is it dead?" the boy gasped.

"Ah no. It belongs to me. I made it." The old man looked very pleased with himself, and drew the object once again from his pocket, he showed it to Duncan. It was a castanet – old and worn, the dancing Spanish lady painted upon it held her hands high, hips swishing the voluminous red dress. With a clench of the fist, the castanet calmed the struggling construct of bones writhing in the hearth. With one more click of the wood, it stopped struggling and lay quite, quite still.

Duncan stepped cautiously back, examining the creature from a safe distance. Would it leap for him? The man unsprung the trap with a gentle hand. Its body was indeed oval, ladybird-like. Its legs still and curled below its abdomen were segmented into three parts. They reminded Duncan of the legs of a crab. It was quite pretty.

The upper two segments resembled the thighbones of a small rodent. The leg ended in a curved bone that had been fashioned into a scimitar-like shape, held together by the tiniest wires, hair-like. Small springs mimicked musculature, tendons and ligaments. They sprouted from a flat underside made of tiny teeth, arranged like plates of armour.

The old man gently cupped the construct to examine it. His expression was so gentle. It was like the way Mummy looked at Duncan.

The boy watched in mute fascination as the man gently turned it over. He produced a tiny needle-like screwdriver from his robe and gently prised open one of the bony plates on its underside. Silently he opened one after another, placing them carefully on the floor in the order he had removed them. As Duncan peered into the construct, a gentle breath escaped his lips as he spied rows of inert cogs of brass and silver. Spring levers. Like the kind you see in a pocket watch. And the beautiful clock on the windowsill.

Satisfied, he replaced the teeth-armour in the same exact order in which he removed them. "Oh, it's wonderful," said Duncan. Thoughts of clockwork trains and the marvels of walking tin robots in the big department stores faded away in comparison with the construct before him. "What does it do?"

"Just a toy. Before I came here, I was a toymaker. I made myself a companion. Do you like it?"

"I think so. I'm not worried anymore," smiled the boy. "Can I help you fix it?"

He watched as the man straightened bent and damaged wires with smooth strokes of thumb and forefinger. His fingers became discoloured with grease. The man took a sideways glance at the wide-eyed boy next to him.

"I think I may have to take it all to pieces now."

"But why?"

"Your mother will not allow it. It would be a shame though."

The old man turned it over gently, picked up the castanet and clicked it once. Slowly the little creature's legs began to twitch, cogs inside spinning into a gentle purr. "Oh!" exclaimed Duncan, his hands reaching out to it.

With a finger upon his lips, the old man hushed him and clicked a rhythm with the castanet. The construct creature became animated, taking a few steps forward, then back, then scuttled up to Duncan's knee.

"Ah now – it appears to like you," the old man whispered. Duncan beamed with delight. If he could borrow the toy, then maybe when his friends came to play in the den they could make up games with the construct.

"And now I must remove it."

Duncan placed a hand on the old man's forearm, alarm etched across his face.

"I must. Your mother would never allow it, and she has been so kind with her hospitality towards me." He smiled, watching as the child's eyes flicked left and right. "We don't have to tell her?" he blurted.

"Ah, you are the man of the house, yes? So you can keep a secret?" He took the boy in – his gaze, his face, his expression. Duncan nodded enthusiastically.

The old man had lived many a lifetime, met many a man, he had experience. He knew how to judge people, to weigh and measure them. He knew the boy would be true to his word – well, for a while at least, but a while was all the time he needed.

Duncan pointed to the smooth thorax of the construct. "What's that?" he asked, indicating a tiny pattern of swirls and symbols intricately carved into the bone.

"You have most sharp eyes. Nothing. A pattern." The

old man sighed. It was time to leave. "Will you look after him for me, until it is healed?"

"Oh yes, yes please!" replied Duncan.

"Our secret?" Duncan nodded. "Then we need to find somewhere soft and warm for him to sit." Duncan followed the old man's gaze as he scanned the room and carried it over to the bed, placing it lovingly upon crumpled sheets.

"There," the old man said, as he stroked the creature's carapace with gentle fingers. The creature scuttled away under Duncan's pillow, which billowed as it nestled itself. The old man turned to the young boy. "Keep it there, warm until it mends. Do not take it out for a day or two or it will become frail again. Our little secret, remember."

Obedience.

Running the back of a forefinger down the young boy's cheek. "You really are a most special child. Return to bed, toy will watch you as you sleep." The boy climbed into bed, the old man drawing up his covers around him. "Sleep, yes?"

"Yes," murmured Duncan. "And thank you for my pet. I will call him Buggy."

"Wonderful," and he gently closed the door ajar, a half-smile creasing his lips.

The young one closed his eyes, shifting upon his mattress. As his mind began to search for Spitfires in a blue ocean sky.

XXVIII

Post haste

James Hendry sucked air sharply through clenched teeth as he crouched down next to the corpse. Poor Hen McGlennon, he had liked the big fellow, always a smile and a quick quip as he passed. Such a shock, all this. So unexpected. He wasn't that old. Big healthy farm lad.

He'd been at home when the call came, urging him to this building, a thrown-together collection of outhouses and sheds at the very edge of the village; along a rough track of weeds and grass that grew tall between the tyre troughs of irregular visits. A barren place of crows and hawks against the shadows of the mountains and the sounds of the loch in the distance. He never had liked the place, and today was no exception.

"Looks like he had one too many and fell?" Face ashen, shock at finding the body, Craig was the first slaughter man in of the day. "His breath smelt of whisky."

"He isn't the only one who's had a drink in here then?" James regretted his words as soon as he uttered them. Poor lad, what was he – sixteen, seventeen? Tall and broad, it was easy to forget his youth. He was nearly as tall as Hen had been, heavier set perhaps. Took after his mother, Highland stock.

Craig bowed his head, awkwardness bringing faint colour to his round face. "It was the fright you see," he whispered eventually. "Never seen a body before. Took a swig after phoning you."

"It's all right, lad, I spoke out of turn. You were entitled to one, we all liked the big man," James said apologetically. "Wonder what happened to him."

Lying peacefully on his back, Hen looked as though he was simply sleeping. Legs slightly bent at the knee, solid boots turned inward, clothes orderly, no evidence that anything untoward had happened. Pressing his fingers into the neck, James tried to find some signs of life, questions racing through his mind. There was no pulse. Had Craig checked? The lad shook his head: "I just knew, you see."

Scanning the room with a practiced eye, the policeman nodded, no evidence of a struggle, no signs of foul play, bar an upturned waste-paper basket and scattered papers. No blood visible on any surface as far as he could see, no scuffmarks or dents. But there was a cricket bat lying on the floor not far from the body. It looked clean, unused in anger.

Nodding towards the meat locker room, he turned to the lad, who stood stock still, eyes never leaving the body lying on the floor of the office.

"Checked in there?"

Craig shook his head, eyes now averted from the body of the night watchman.

"So was that it then? A few too many and a bang on the head… then it was all over? No one to help him? Or hear?" Craig's voice broke then, shock replaced by grief. Placing his hand on the young man's shoulder, the policeman motioned him to sit down in the only chair. The lad's legs buckled and he fell heavily back into the chair, head between his knees as sobs wracked his body.

Turning back to the body, the policeman noticed a large discoloured lump on the forehead, partially concealed by hair, but no blood, the skin unbroken. No tears in the clothing. Peaceful-like. James had seen many a broken crown on the streets of Glasgow in his time, heads caved in by blunt objects too, but this didn't resemble any of them.

One of Sillitoe's he'd been, big strong Jim from the rural outcrops of the Highlands. It had been a shock at first. An eye opener – brought in to tackle the razor gangs. July 1939 it was, when the Beehive Boys and the South Side Sticker combined, stoning the force as they arrived in Thistle Street in squad cars and vans. Shop windows were smashed and his job was to stand guard to prevent looting.

Came for the Glasgow smile.

Poor Hen. Nothing as violent as that, lying there with only the carcasses for company. No wound by knife or glass making that cut from the corners of the mouth to the ears. A vile scar in the shape of a smile. He'd been gone from those streets for years but you never forgot the damage a razor did to a face.

He unbuttoned the man's collar, feeling the cold beneath his fingertips and for a moment the tenuousness of mortality swept over him. The whole here today, gone tomorrowness of it all. He hadn't planned on this posting being anything other than a slow slipping into comfortable retirement: farm squabbles, the occasional poacher. But not a death. Poor wretch. This was a job for a doctor. Autopsy and then the church took over. Service, flowers, grieving. He would have to visit Hen's wife. What would she do now without a weekly wage and such a large family to feed?

Opening the collar he noticed something strange about the veins in the neck. Taking a pencil from his top pocket, he traced the carotid, then the jugular. The blood vessels were prominent and black, as if filled with ink. Rigid. James frowned. True, he had no medical training to speak of, but this was surely an oddity. They protruded from the man's neck. Checking the forearms, he saw the same. This was beyond his expertise.

"What is it?" the boy ventured.

James ignored the young man's words. Instead, calmly told him to phone Lonnie Gray, the owner. "We'll need to speak to him." Scanning the room again, something else didn't seem right. Something slightly amiss. Out of kilter. What was it?

He felt it scratching at his years of experience. That odd sense of déjà vu one occasionally got. A nagging feeling that you had missed something obvious and important.

Then it suddenly dawned… heart attack victims didn't lie down, arms neatly arranged by their sides in their final moments. They surely didn't have raised and blackened veins.

James rose, puzzled by this mystery. The doctor should surely be here soon. And Lonnie. He needed other eyes and ears. A sharp pain twinged through his protesting knees, too many years chasing criminals over the cobbles. *You're getting old*, he thought. Where did it go? Those days and years. Waking each morning with that unending hope. Got through the day with an expectation of something. And yet when the time came to sleep, left with the grimness of reality. That ahead, stretched the endless tomorrows of other people's failures and mistakes written down on a notebook in your pocket.

"Come on, lad, let's do a turn of the outside, see what we can see. I need your young eyes." Craig looked relieved to be leaving the room with its metallic taint and the body of his friend. And if he was honest, James was ready to escape the unease within the room.

The sun was climbing in a clear sky, tinting the grey walls of the building faint sepia. It was going to be a beautiful day, no rain in the distance, but not a happy one. He knew he had to inspect the pens where the cattle would be herded, but he was reluctant to leave the lad for the moment.

The sound of a car approaching drove James to his

feet. Doctor Rigby. The Morris drew parallel to them, caked with an aftermath of grass and small puddles. Reaching for his bag the doctor stepped out into the courtyard. The policeman noticed he was tired, slightly unkempt, a three-day growth and a tie that showed food stains. He motioned the doctor to enter the building, out of earshot of Craig who still sat with his head in his hands.

Following, but leaving the doctor to do a thorough examination, James went into the meat locker. The smell was overwhelming despite it being cooler than the main office, and he wondered if the refrigeration had somehow failed during the night. Poorly lit, he searched for a light switch, springing into sharp focus stained tiles lining the walls and the floor, grouting blackened with waste. Two deep basins sat against the farthest wall, one on either side of the slab. Several carcasses stretched from metal pinions. Placing his handkerchief across his nose and mouth he moved further into the room.

There was liquid on the floor, a dull metallic sheen to it. The small bulbs in the walls threw odd shadows into corners he couldn't see. But nowhere for an intruder to hide. He wondered how anyone could work here, surrounded by the dying and the dead animals, stripped and hung and gutted. *A sad beginning for your Sunday dinner*, he thought bleakly.

He was glad to leave the room, shutting the metal door firmly behind him and stood at the entrance, where the freshness of the day whipped away the taste of metal from his throat. He waited silently as the doctor phoned for the body to be taken back for autopsy. Once that had happened he would wait for Lonnie. Final check and then write up his report. His stomach reminded him that he had skipped breakfast.

Before she died, his wife would have made him a quick flask and sandwich. Tongue or home-cured ham. So sudden it had been. Such pain within her that she would lie beside him in their bedroom at night and try to muffle her tears. Just weeks from beginning to casket. Such flowers that brimmed over the sides and across the pallbearers shoulders, like pale tears.

It had taken him a long time to forgive the Church with its endless promises of an afterlife. He would have preferred a current life with her for a few more years. A few at least. They had only had each other. No children had blessed their union, and that had caused her so much anguish. She had endlessly blamed herself despite his attempts to assure her that she was all that mattered to him. Since then he hadn't really lived. Simply existed in the cracks of memories.

Interrupted by the sound of the van arriving to collect the body of his friend, he talked briefly to the driver and nodded as the doctor and the van left. There was little more he could do now, apart from making sure Craig had company until the owner arrived.

Poor lad. What a way to start his day.

After the chill of the meat locker, he was relieved to feel the sun on his back. His scalp was sweating and he felt the familiar trickle of sweat on his forehead. Stopping to remove his helmet, he wiped his brow. As he did so, he noticed a patch of earth beneath the window of the office was reddened. No clay earth hereabouts. Taking a closer look, he could barely make out what the cause was. It was small and matted. Something dead or dying in the weeds?

Too large for a rat, too small for a fox. A ginger-coloured object. He very nearly moved on until he saw the gash in the chest – not the work of scavengers nor birds this. The body was covered head to toe with angry-looking red lumps and there were puncture marks between, leaking brackish liquid and a gaping wound where the heart should have been.

"It's Gas Bottle!" Startled by the silent approach and outburst of the young lad,

James cast him a quizzical look.

"Hen's cat. Gas Bottle. What's happened to it?"

"Foxes I would think, lad."

Neither man had the heart to leave the poor thing there in this heat. The stench would be unbearable by midday. Not as bad as that of dead hedgehogs though. "Get us a spade will you lad?" As Craig ambled off in the direction of the animal pens and the storeroom, James kept an ear out for the sound of Lonnie's car. He was certainly taking his time. All the policeman wanted was for this day to end. To put his feet up and listen to the wireless.

Craig lifted the stiff cat on the shovel, gingerly holding it away from him, and asked James what they should do with it.

179

"Furnace?"

As he nodded in agreement, James suddenly placed a hand on the young man's arm. "Hang on. Stop Craig." The matted cat fur began to bubble on the extended spade. Pustules exploded from the matted mess throwing bloody puss onto the men. Craig hurled the shovel away from him as both men staggered back in disgust.

He didn't like this, didn't like this at all. The whole day had an "off" feel. Skewed.

A creeping feeling began to burrow its way inside him that he had been gravely mistaken about Hen.

XXIX

Gone

She was making some toast early that morning. Starlings and finches twitching the trees, scuttling for worms beyond the window that freshly curtained, was open to let in the air. Their guest walked into the room. He had been quiet recently, taking his meals in his room and she was worried that he was embarrassed to be in her company after the incident with the Major. But not at all, he had said when she apologised. He had things that needed his attention.

There was some small relief in that, she supposed, and offered him tea.

Would he like an egg for breakfast, a three-minute one

was always just right or perhaps some porridge in case it turned chilly?He bowed his head and said no thank you; he would be gone for the day and possibly may not return that evening. She felt flustered. What if she didn't hear the door, what if he was left alone on the doorstep while she slept soundly? Perhaps she could give him a spare key? *Well of course*, she thought, *that is what hotels do.*

It was rather bulky and attached to a thin chain, which he slipped into one of the endless pockets within the great coat. He had on a red tartan scarf today and he said he was determined to adapt to the traditions. His long hair was tucked inside his hat again and she thought he looked like a jovial Father Christmas, even though it was September.

When she had said goodbye she wandered upstairs to kiss her child awake. Rumpled, he had tossed his covers off and lay sprawled across his bed. His cheeks looked flushed and she felt his forehead for a fever. He was hot beneath her palm, and his breathing felt uneven. Gently she cradled him and raised him up. His eyelids fluttered and for a moment between sleep and waking she saw phantoms chase across his eyes until he focused on her face.

She propped him up with pillows, and said she would nip and get him some Friar's Balsam in hot water. They would steam his fever out of him and then she would sit with him while he went back to sleep.

The cream bowl was heavy. It had been used a long time ago to make jelly moulds, but today it would have a medicinal use. Passing the door to the dining room she noticed there was a draught blowing through. It knocked the door against the jamb with a repetitive bumping. Puzzled, she set down the bowl and the towel, and pulled the door tightly into the frame, turning the key. There. How annoying!

His breathing eased under the towel she draped over his head, the bowl under his nose with the balsam helping his cough and he started to relax.

"There now," she said, "Much better my love. Try and sleep."

Satisfied he would doze for an hour or so, she tidied his covers, put the toys away and checked that windows were tightly shut.

Trying not to spill the remains of the balsam, she tucked the towel under her arm. Soup. Soup was ideal for poorly boys. She could boil some vegetables and use their water to make chicken soup with the stock she had stored earlier that week. Possibly some barley to thicken it, and corn flour. She really needed to make an inventory of jars and pickles sat high up on the shelves of the larder. Jams didn't go off did they?

The door to the dining room was ajar and she frowned, surely she had locked it? There was too much of value in there and she couldn't risk anything being stolen. She pulled it closed again. Perhaps she should get the door seen to by a joiner. Old houses. So many problems.

She put everything down on the kitchen table, and got out the ingredients for the soup. Pan of water boiling on the stove and a small amount of salt to give it a nip. The larder was narrow and squat but quite easy to organise.

Empty Mason jars and lids, tureens and jelly moulds. Pans for stew and soups. All found in cupboards. There were labels on some of the glass jars – tomatoes 1938, blackcurrant jam 1937, and marmalade 1938. Such a long life ago, when Gordon was with her and their baby just a whisper and a dream.

Perhaps ten years was rather a long time to keep jellied goods, but she'd have a taste and then decide. A draught blew around her ankles, distracting her from unscrewing the lid off the jam. It would suck all the heat from the kitchen if she didn't go and close the door.

Perhaps the draught whistled down the chimney into hearths standing empty for so many years. No servants now to lay the fires in each of the rooms. So many gone to those *"once more over the top lads."* Yet smoke was so lovely when it drifted from rooftops and away. There was coal aplenty in the outhouse. She would take the scuttles in the morning and fill each one.

But placing her hand beneath the opening she felt no draught at all. Was it coming under the door that led into the garden? Looking through the window she saw no movement in the trees. It was as still as a summer's day should be.

Where else then?

The kitchen door swung open so suddenly it made her start. She froze by the sink, staring into the narrow hallway. Had she not bolted the front door? It was gloomy there. Trophies peered down at the everlasting tiles that patterned towards her and she could hardly breathe.

What could they see with their taxidermied eyes that she couldn't? All was so still, except for the draught that gathered force and lifted her apron around her waist.

Servant's bells with rooms and names began to ring above the larder door, clamours waking her from seizures of nothingness. Bells in copper filled the empty hallway with their sounds. Butler's pantry, first bedroom, third bedroom, madam, landing, cellar, howling for her attention as they would any servant below stairs. Demanding, deafening.

She squatted down near the table, hiding away amidst the wood. Would it stop? Or would it continue forever until all she would see was the blood behind her eyelids and the sounds that resonated through her to the cellar?

Till.

As abruptly as it had started, it ceased. Cautiously she stood up, adjusting her apron and her skirt. She glanced around the room. The bells were still quivering, but silent. For a moment she stayed where she was, listening with that aftershock of the unexpected.

It may have been five minutes, or ten, she wasn't sure – before she went to check that the front door was closed. Such an old and sagging house, peeling away its history in layers. Ivy and shingles, wallpaper and mould, whitewash and parquet that needed replacing. Dust seemed to hold it together and the more she dusted and cleaned the more she unearthed that which was dying.

Locked. Not bolted, but locked. She checked it several times to reassure herself. When Gordon was with her, he would be wonderful in such situations. Calm in the face of a storm, she used to say and he would smile in that bashful way of his and take her hand. Would he be proud of her courage, even though it often wavered?

The dining room door was ajar again, the room dark because she had drawn the curtains the night before. Switching on one of the lamps on an occasional table, the large table dominated the room; chairs upholstered and pushed neatly along its length.

Of the contents of the sideboard she had so excitedly laid out on the table, there was no sign. No silverware, plates or cutlery, no linens or cloths. Dust had been disturbed but that was all that rested on the rectagonal surface. Flustered, she wondered if for a moment her child had put them back, but the sideboard cupboards were empty. Throwing back the curtains, she checked for broken glass or a catch that had been forced.

For once she reacted not with anxiety or panic, but with a clear and sharp anger.

She found herself shouting at the emptiness, calling for them to reveal themselves. Had they no shame after the war years? Had they no sense of compassion or care?

"Mummy?" standing in the doorway, small lip trembling, hair at odds with his scalp. And she felt guilty. For bringing him here, for isolating him. For new beginnings that perhaps were in the end too much for her. She scooped him up and held him, closing the door angrily, unaware of the small blue voyeur crawling from its hiding place.

XXX

The Doctor

Splashing cold water onto his face, he looked into the eyes before him. Tired – brown, bloodshot threads, dark circles and generous bags. Lines about his mouth earned not from laughter but too many battlefield surgeries. He wondered how many European mirrors told their observers the same story.

He dragged his eyes away from the depressing sight, glancing beyond at the reflection of the small room behind him. Private chambers, a small space to get away from it all.

Such a poor night's sleep before the call to the abattoir and the body of Hen. He doubted tonight would be any different.

Four walls of bile-green paint for study, rest, even sleep when his mind had exhausted the pain. An afterthought added to the original consultancy room. Primitive medicine, he thought grimly, but his eyes were drawn reluctantly to the slab and a cold white sheet.

The man had been a friend. A few laughs in the pub, Christmas, Hogmanay, church, the usual visits to the surgery for a man of his age. He knew the family well, had delivered their first born in their front room. Delivered all of them in fact. Brave woman. No pain relief. Sturdy stock these Highland women.

His thoughts were interrupted by a heavy knock at the door. During the ticking seconds of a polite pause, he dried himself on clean white cotton, folded the towel and placed it in the metal ring screwed into the wall next to the hand basin. He straightened his tie, noticing the stains. "You need a woman about the place," he chided himself.

"In here," he called, turning to greet James.

"Well?" the officer enquired.

"To be honest Jim, I really have no idea."

"Really... no idea?"

"I saw things in Europe, men with an endless need for... methods... Grimness. In Berlin there were things... sights, horrors. But this... it's like all and none of them. This is beyond me."

Discomfort interrupted the men. That awkward envelope of words unsaid.

"I see." The officer sighed. "Anything in your books?"

"Not much cause for the more exotic of ailments in a Highland village I'm afraid."

"The smell too?"

"Ach you can still smell it? Him, I'm afraid. Be thankful Mrs Grey had so many candles in stock."

James smiled weakly as the old doctor swept his arm at the numerous scented candles sitting on saucers and jar lids around the room.

"That's not normal, is it?"

"No." Malcolm shook his head. "It's not," he said flatly.

"Let's be getting on with it then," James sighed.

James nodded and the doctor pulled back the sheet. He could not help the sharp intake of breath at the sight of big Hen's corpse. Since that morning of its discovery, it was much changed.

Whatever was being released by the body soon settled on James' taste buds. He felt his tongue quiver with revulsion. He fought hard to stop himself from gagging. The taste was vile, sickly sweet like rotten fruit mixed with honey, laden with a vomit burn and a hint of almond. He pulled a handkerchief from his pocket as fast as his fingers were able, wishing he had a menthol lozenge. He held his hand up in apology to the doctor, who merely shrugged. "Jim, I vomited after the changes of the body."

And what a change. What his eyes were showing him now was a million miles away from how they had viewed Hen the morning of his discovery. The skin was now a pale lilac colour, unwrinkled and smooth, wax-like. Small droplets of clear moisture sat on its surface, unmoving, as if Hen had been sweating. But the worst part was the veins.

It was as if every blood vessel had risen to the surface, a crisscross spider's web of black threads covered the corpse. His lips appeared to have shrunk, pulled away from the mouth revealing sickly black gums and tombstone teeth. It gave the corpse an unnerving snarl. The eyeballs were enlarged, his closed eyelids barely able to contain the bloating.

"What…" was all James could utter.

Malcolm just shook his head. "Wait for this, it gets worse."

James shot him a questioning glance. "The blood, it's black like tar and strange, congealed like the consistency of jam. It doesn't flow. And the flesh Jim, globular, rubbery almost – closest thing I can think of is blubber."

"You cut him?"

Malcolm sighed. "Didn't need to, just look at this."

James followed as the doctor moved to the end of the table and rolled up the sheet around his feet. "Observe," he gestured. From the heel to the toes, both of Hen's feet were wrapped in a white cloth bandage, no trace of blood. On the left foot the bandage was sealed with some kind of cream cement.

Malcolm pulled on a pair of rubber gloves and began to slowly unravel the bandage. There, along the top of the foot, a thin rectangle of skin and flesh had been removed. James peered into the wound expecting to see bone. But there was nothing. Just a hole surrounded by the strange lilac flesh just as the doctor described. The bone had been removed.

"What the devil is going on here?" James said, shaking.

"There's more… the knees, cartilage, left knee cap. Gone. And I don't mean just hacked out. This was surgical skill, precise, to leave the leg so intact. Almost to preserve the body, with as little damage as possible. His heart, Jim. His heart is missing. You may need to see this."

James waved the suggestion away. "I'll take your word for it. I need outside help with this." He ran his hand through his hair and shook his head. He was lost. This was a nightmare. Things like this didn't happen in real life, especially not in small villages in the Highlands. Malcolm covered the corpse and then went to his chair and sat down wearily.

"My best guess?" He sighed. "Someone administered some kind of poison or toxin into poor Hen's system, God knows how, no discernible markers I can see. He died. They took a scalpel to him; with considerable skill they removed bone and tissue. They wrapped the wounds in bandages, sealed them with some kind of cement, I'm guessing, to keep in the smell, because there's no chance of blood loss with that damn tar in his veins. Maybe they were not sure how long it would be before the body was discovered. How, with what, I've got no damn clue. I suggest you tell as many folk as you can to lock the doors and windows. If whoever did this is still around then we are in trouble, we are all in serious trouble."

XXXI

Locks

"And even though we are a safe village, it may be wise to lock your doors and windows for the time being." It had been a hectic and unpleasant couple of days for James; death, suicide and now this report of a burglary at Loch House. The rosy retirement he had imagined on leaving the streets of Glasgow, paling now into an elusive pipe dream.

When he arrived, Annette met him at the front door. Anxiety clouded her face and he could see the fear and tension in her small frame; altogether a different woman from the one he had met at the church. At her side was her child, tear stained and clutching her hand. He could see she was trying to compose herself, straightening her housecoat and smoothing her hair, yet her voice was thin and cracked and deep bruises had formed beneath her eyes. As she asked him to come in, he was struck by how terribly dark it was within, so little natural light reached into this hallway crowded with heavy furniture and the glass gazes of deer and pheasant.

She showed him into the dining room. The long sideboard stood against the opposite wall, behind a dining table and chairs. Again there was that sense of dark heaviness within this room, furniture and fittings that came from another age.

He made notes as she told him about the wind that she thought had come from a door or window being opened, and the contents of the sideboard being taken. Her confusion and worry was palpable in the way she twisted the wedding ring endlessly round and round her finger.

Thanking her for the offer of a drink, he said he had best be off and write up the case. As he left he asked her if she would mind if he came over in the early evening to check on the house again.

Supper that night was a solemn affair. Duncan was tired, and their guest had asked if he might take his meal in his room as he had letters he wished to write. In a way Annette found this a relief.

When the house was quiet and still, she wandered through the downstairs rooms.

She had secured the windows and doors earlier when the police sergeant had returned, true to his word. He was a kind man and she had been grateful to have someone to talk to about her worries, not for herself oddly enough, but for her child.

Lying in her bed she picked up a book and read a couple of chapters before she finally dozed off, the night-light burning quietly beside her. She found it comforting these days to have it on.

At some stage her sleep was disturbed. She saw the night-light send shadows across the room and she realised her cover had fallen off the bed. Slipping her feet into slippers and throwing a gown around her shoulders she made her way onto the landing. All was quiet from the rooms of her child and the guest. Their doors were closed.

She looked over the balustrade into the hallway. Pausing for a moment she descended the stairs and put the light on. The frill around the shade made spidery shapes on the wallpaper. The front door was bolted, the key in place and she assumed it was the chill that had woken her.

Boiling milk to pour upon the cocoa powder, she tucked her hair behind her ears absently. It curled against her will, stubbornly refusing to remain in a bun or a plait. Her reflection gazed back at her from the window above the sink. She had lost weight in the last weeks and her cheekbones were too sharp. Her dresses hung on her and she had tried to belt them tighter, but knew she would have to tuck and nip them. She should have asked Nora for help with that when she had stayed there, but that hadn't crossed her mind.

She put a full teaspoon of sugar into the hot cocoa. She must build herself up a bit. She would be no good to

Duncan if she were ill. As she switched off the lights in the kitchen she made sure the doors were closed tight behind her. They were. Tight and locked, keys on a heavy chain she had kept on the side table beside her bed.

XXXII

Clocks

Time was a funny thing, he thought, staring up at the ceiling above his bed. It wasn't any particular colour or shape. It didn't sound like anything or have a smell. Not like the shadowy bits in the coalhouse that Mummy said were maybe rat droppings. No. Time was a strange fellow. It happened whether you told it to or not. It happened in clocks, seasons, and the weather over the moors, the moon. Happened so you had to wear a jumper but not a scarf. Told you when to go to bed or have your tea. Time was a naughty boy whom adults couldn't punish.

The nighttime flitted across the metal patterns in the ceiling, finding the odd edge and coving.

Time was trapped in the wristwatch he had found in the little side table drawer in his bedroom. It had a leather strap, like Daddy's.

He thought a lot about time at the moment. He had a lot of it on his hands until school started again on Monday and that made him giggle because he had made up his own pun.

Sometimes time just wasn't, like when he was very busy, or when he was asleep. You just were or you weren't. If you had bad dreams then time gathered speed the next day and you were tired and poorly.

*

He thought he would play with his train set for a while and then venture out into the coal shed. Perhaps if he pushed the wood back a bit he could climb through the hole. If it were big enough he would have a den, with special treasures in there for safekeeping. A blanket and a candle. And then when Bertie came over he would be very impressed by it all. Then he decided he would do that first. Popping Buggy inside his jumper he whispered that they were on an adventure and Buggy wriggled a bit. Duncan thought the toy was maybe more excited than he was.

It was very heavy, and he was a bit worried that it would fall on him, but then he remembered the bravery from the night before, and he braced himself. It moved ever so slightly, he was sure. Over to the right there was enough of a gap now and he peered down and looked through. It was very, very dark. He couldn't even see if the track marks disappeared into it. A torch. He would need one.

He took the torch from the kitchen drawer. It was rubber and had belonged to his daddy. Mummy said it was a useful thing to have in case the electricity went off. He wasn't sure how he would feel if all the lights went off, but Mummy had said it would be cosy and nothing to worry about.

The beam was long and strong and would be perfect for the den adventure. He began to wriggle through the gap in the coalhouse wall. It wasn't a door and no mice had made it.

It felt a bit crumbly under his palms and he worried that he might scuff his shoes. But he was an adventurer and what he would find on the other side of the wall would, he was sure, make it a lovely expedition.

As he was halfway through he heard the sound of Annette calling him. He was a good boy. He knew that. But just for once he was going to be as quiet as a mouse.

And hide. With Buggy.

The torch beam was powerful like a lighthouse beacon plunging across the blackness of the waters to save the sailors from the wreck on the rocks. Duncan saw this room was much, much smaller than the coal shed and empty save for a small fireplace and grate that jutted out into the earth floor. He couldn't see all of it though. Just the fireplace part, but it smelt funny, like the smell Mummy had mentioned in the coal shed and the larder. It made him wrinkle his nose, but he pushed himself through the gap with determination. Explorers never gave up. His shorts caught on a bit of wood and he loosened them carefully. Explorers were always smart and took care of their things. He was a bit worried that he would hurt Buggy, so he took him out and popped him on the floor in front of him. Buggy wriggled in his funny wiggly way and trotted off in front of Duncan, the little metal ladybird feet scratching on the floor.

Once through, he stood up and shone the light around the room. He felt rather proud of himself. Expecting emptiness, his mouth gaped at the sight.

What were all the things from the sideboard doing in here?

XXXIII

Wildflowers

The sun began to fall behind the house, the bright shine of this day now fading. Annette took a walk across the lawn to the end of the driveway. Grass knee-high, but she had stopped fretting about this. She had thought that perhaps sheep or the cows that weren't allowed in the churchyard might be useful? With that she headed for the gate. Duncan had come in from the outhouses and had insisted he stay and wash the dishes for her and lay the table while she went and gathered wildflowers. Where had her baby gone, she wondered. Grown and growing.

Long trousers soon.

They were abundant in the hedgerows, a riot of colour,

perfect for the kitchen. The scissors lay small in her apron pocket, and she had forgotten to bring a basket, but her arms would do. The temperature was dropping and she thought about returning for a coat when she heard a greeting called from beyond the gates.

He waved. Uniform pressed, his helmet on his head, buttons and badges shining.

"I was just passing and thought I'd drop by to see if all was well?"

She hadn't seen him approach, or heard him. Bicycles tended to be quieter than cars, she mocked within her head and smiled at the return of a humour she had all but forgotten she had.

She hurried the last few yards and opened the gate. Standing there in the fall of the day they may have looked like sweethearts to a passerby. However, they were, she thought, becoming friends. She enjoyed his company, calm and considerate. A solid shoulder. Odd that she had never seen him with his wife. Perhaps she wasn't a churchgoer.

She thanked him for dropping by and no, there hadn't been any other incidents but she had taken his advice and ordered a telephone to be installed in the Lodge. It may take some time, but she was grateful for the fact he had suggested it. Would he like to come up to the house for a cup of tea? She had made some scones that very morning. Surprised by a look of doubt that suddenly changed his expression, she wondered briefly if she had been too forward. She wouldn't like to have given him the wrong impression.

"That would be lovely. Thank you," he said and they walked back up the drive together.

Sitting in the kitchen seemed to have become a habit for her these days. The other rooms were so filled with furniture that was dark and heavy and outdated, and more and more she felt overwhelmed at the thought of cleaning and dusting and painting. Dolly had kindly said she would help, but Annette knew she had her own job as a housekeeper to a man in the village, and she was also looking after Albert.

The policeman had taken off his helmet and placed it on a spare chair near him. They sat in amicable silence drinking their tea and he complimented her on her baking.

She wanted to ask him about the poor man Dolly had said died suddenly. She didn't know the man or his family but Dolly had said it had caused quite a stir in the village. There was talk about a heart attack. But whatever the cause of his death she would have to wait for Dolly to give her more details rather than question this man. It was improper really to be so inquisitive about such a sad occurrence.

So she didn't.

The front door opening interrupted her thoughts; hinges that needed oiling making a sound that set your teeth on edge. She felt suddenly quite embarrassed by this, by the age of the house, by the signs of neglect and emptiness, aware that in the policeman's eyes she must lack the social graces and funds that this house had been accustomed to.

As the elderly guest knocked politely on the door, James turned and locked eyes with the old man. There passed something strange between the two men. It was so fleeting, less than a second, yet Annette felt a cooling in the atmosphere of afternoon tea and scones.

"Oh – Mr Hendry. This is our guest. He has been staying here whilst he looks for other lodgings." The men nodded to each other as the policeman gathered his hat and thanked Annette for her courtesy. "Do come again." she smiled and walked him to the door.

Behind her she heard the guest mount the stairs to his room, the sound of his door quietly closing.

XXXIV

Fairies

Duncan sped through a land of dreams astride the first of three carriages of red polished wood. Bare feet trailed through blades of tall grass woven in silk. His navy dressing gown tied tightly over freshly pressed pajamas. Buggy nestled in his pocket. He laughed and whooped as he sped along, waving merrily at the giant bunnies hopping amongst sunflowers as the Spitfires looped the loop above him in the crystal blue.

The train chased a tiny fluorescent light, a friendly fairy, or butterfly perhaps. As they crested the hill the engine slowed, and the nursery rhyme sun rose and smiled at him. Then – whoosh! – off they went speeding down the other side of the hill, the boy laughing with glee at the sudden speed.

Off he went through the long, long grass, towards the distance and that dark barrier looming like a wall stretched so tightly along the horizon. He shifted on the carriage, wanting to get off now but it was too fast. Too fast. He couldn't even turn around to find the rabbits and the lovely fields because the wind gathered his gown and whipped it behind him pushing him forwards and onwards to the darkening place.

He thought about jumping but knew he would hurt himself and blood made him sicky. Then the train lurched, wheels squealed in protest as the engine braked. And he was there. Just there. Stopped at the barrier. It scared him but he wasn't sure why. He thought Buggy might know as he gently pulled his little creature out of the pocket where it had lain so still and soft.

The train engine cooled and clicked like the legs of his pet as he clambered down and looked at the wall. Reaching out to it he wondered why it blocked their path. Did the rails go beyond it? Far away into a distance like in the films they used to watch in the cinema on the next street to where they lived before it was bombed in the Blitz.

It wasn't a wall at all but a very, very tall hedge. Much taller than he; neatly trimmed flat edges with a flat top. The little fairy buzzed beside it just out of reach of his outstretched hand. He felt it was his friend. Travelling with him as it had through the fields and the flowers and the colour. Curiosity won the battle with fear and he dismounted the carriage.

He walked over towards it, the light from the wings hovered closer. He could see it clearly now. It looked like the little baby thing he found in the chocolate man's box, body covered in a smooth fluorescent blue fur. Dragonfly wings buzzed from its shoulders, colours constantly changing like oil on water. Its tiny face flashed him a warm, friendly toothpaste smile, welcoming eyes, feline amber under the small curling horns at its brow. Warm honey colours.

"Hello my Duncan."

He felt Buggy shift slightly, digging shard pincers into his palm.

"Are you a fairy?"

"Yes! Yes that's exactly what I am; you are such a clever boy. Would you care to name me?"

Duncan smiled gently at the praise, the embers of fear still smouldering within his young heart.

"But how can I?"

The hedge wall towering about them. He felt it move just beyond his reach.

The fairy froze in movement, weighing the young boy up. "You may call me Dybbuk if you wish…"

Nodding. "I don't like it here," *Duncan said finally.* "I think I want to go home now," *and turned towards that beautiful engine, seeing it slumped now upon its tracks, wheels flopping over the rails as if melted. He searched the landscape for bunnies to rescue them but none could be seen and the sky above was empty of those shining Spitfires. Even the sun was retreating, darkening as nighttime was hurrying.*

The dybbuk hovered in front of him.

"Let me show you the way home then," *pointing to an arch in the hedgerow that materialised, misty and hesitant.*

The aperture was dark, the interior shrouded in shadow. There was a strangely powerful smell, both sweet and rotten like windfalls in wet summers.

"I don't want to," he said finally.

Spreading his wings, the fairy tilted his small, pointed chin. "But the train has ended, can you not agree? It did such a job for us, what an adventure in wood."

Duncan looked about him. The silk grass still spread out behind them as far as his keen eyes could see, but no bunnies or Spitfires. He looked back at the train. It looked sad drooping on the rails. It was obviously never going to go anywhere ever again.

Duncan stood for a moment and gazed around him, he was lost and alone, he was starting to feel hungry and he really didn't want to miss his breakfast or his mummy may be cross with him. Besides, the dybbuk was his friend now and he had Buggy with him to protect him. He was a big boy now, the man of the house his mummy said and a very brave boy.

With that in his heart, they stepped into the dark.

Duncan did not like what he found on the other side. It was as if he had stepped from day into night. The dybbuk flittered ahead: the only light. Pale lilac and flickering. Like a match. Except he knew not to play with matches.

Didn't he.

It was different to the gap through which he passed into his den; this passageway was walled by a thick, tall hedge, whose edges were rough and thorny. They stretched along

207

as far as his eyes could see in the gloom, narrowing like an arrow. Like Robin Hood. Or that man who shot an apple off the little boy's head. Now what was his name?

There was no grass beneath his bare soles, just dirt and grit, sharp rocks and twigs. He felt their sharpness but knew he could not stop. Thick roots, tree-like, snaked from one side of the tunnel to the other. Strange noises assailed him: animal growls and hoots like distant owls.

Rustlings twitched within the hedge and he felt a sliding before him like rain so fast on a window that wiping it with your hand wouldn't slow it, blurring the really there and the really not. And all the while the dybbuk's light ahead of him, glancing off snake scale and claw, dull green and savage. Keeping him safe.

He could just make out other arches in the hedge set at intervals, between layered stone bird baths and statues of fauns. They were gloomy and inky and he didn't want the dybbuk to take him through them. He wanted to go back now, but the archway through which he came was no more when he turned to look back.

All was sliding and slippy.

He gripped Buggy fearfully. He wanted to go home now. He didn't like it anymore. And he called this, but not loudly because of the rustlings and eyes in the hedgings.

"No way back now..." the dybbuk whispered. But the whisper felt sharp in his ears, like the thorns beneath his feet. Mummy always said to wear your slippers, and he had forgotten.

Just when it was most important.

Taking a few careful steps over roots, he tried to ignore

the noise of leaves drumming faster and louder around him, keeping his eyes on the friendly blue flickering ahead.

Like lightning, but not.

The dybbuk drifted onwards dipping in and out of unfelt currents of wind, and Duncan followed, desperate to keep near the glow of his new friend's blue light. Eyes forward. Always forward; never daring to look fully at the horrors that scurried, crawled or slithered in the undergrowth alongside them.

Stopping suddenly. "Here," said the small fairy creature. "Here it is," and turning to look directly at the young boy with eyes so big. So big, like a bush baby's. Big and round and amber. Lilac pulsed from it like a halo around the head of Jesus in the picture Mummy had found and put above his bed.

Buggy began to move in his pocket, the clicks and scratching becoming more urgent as there, up ahead, rounding a corner that Duncan hadn't noticed in this gloaming, came shadows.

One was that of a man in a hat, long coat, legs spaced wide, long hair flowing in a breeze that unsettled the hedge leaves and branches. The other was long and low and still.

"Who's that?" cried Duncan, backing away from the arch as Buggy frantically scratched at the fabric, the clickings high pitched and screaming.

"Tis no one, just shadows," the dybbuk fluttered. "No one here. Tis the tricks of the maze."

"I want to go home now. Buggy is frightened. And I want my mummy."

Uttering a response in a tongue the boy did not understand, the halo light paled as the hedge to the right shook violently. Wood snapped as heaviness pushed itself through the roots, away from the shadow of the man who turned towards the boy and the dybbuk. Duncan recoiled in horror as a shape the size of a large dog morphed. Oval toad-like head took shape as it entered the dybbuck's light, its face cracked open showing a great maw of small triangular teeth. Dark green skin, gnarly like old tree bark. Open sores and scabs wept blood and sickly liquids flowed across its skin. Limbs were tiny, wasted, ending in warped fingers and claws that propelled its body forward with agonising slowness.

Towards him.

"Monsters..." screamed Duncan, backing away as a long, snake-like tongue flicked from the creature's jaw. Pink and glistening, tip forked like a dragon, swishing on goitered limbs to latch onto the young boy's leg. Painfully slowly on tiny limbs the thing edged its slug-like body closer and closer, when the man stepped out into the light, face blurred with a fog that Duncan didn't want to look through.

It became too much and he turned, holding Buggy tightly in his hand as it clawed at his skin and bit his palms. Runrun Buggy, runrun away from the monsters.

Runrun... faster and faster he ran, through passageways that twisted and wove beneath branches that lapped him and clutched at his jumper till his feet hurt and the tears that his bravery had stopped poured endlessly down his cheeks.

Until.

"Stop..." fluttered the dybbuk. "Stopstop little boy." Wings folding inwards, flashing so fast that the lilac dazzled the passageway and in an instant a column of sunshine cracked the wall of the hedge.

"Swift," urged the dybbuk and flew through the gap. Duncan followed with Buggy clasped tight, glancing back once as the shadow man stretched out his arms and whispered.

"Perfect child."

This passage was filled with sunshine, grass and flowers replacing dirt and grime. Bunnies hopped amongst them. Duncan stared back at the man, his arms stretched out as if pleading for his embrace. Duncan stepped into the light, away from the man, into a small circular space filled with scents of wild flowers, lavender and rose. The sun shone on his face and he heard the aperture through which he came grind shut. Buggy had stilled, then slept. Exhausted. He hoped it wasn't broken – the old man would be cross with him if it was.

The dybbuk, bright now and swaying, called to him, "Come, come, this is the way out."

He felt warmth flow from the tiny creature. "This way." Through the garden he followed the dybbuk as it flitted in and out of a small breeze. Here was all sunshine and flowers and colours and scents. Here was lovely, he thought. Perhaps he would come back again, but with Mummy.

Rounding a corner Duncan stopped in surprise. A window? There, a few paces ahead, was a dead end, but not of neatly cut privet, but a window. His window. Closed to a summer's day.

"Yes," said the dybbuk. "For all you have to do for us to leave is open the window."

"It's my window?"

"Yes it is. And this is your maze."

A puzzled look crossed the boy's features. He shrugged and went to the window, simply flicked the catch and opened it.

*

Duncan woke slowly, hearing his mother call his name. He sat up and rubbed his eyes that seemed sluggish and heavy. His blanket had fallen to the floor and he felt chilly. Maybe he needed his dressing gown and slippers this morning.

Finally clearing the sleep from his eyes, as full consciousness found him, he shivered. There was a breeze. It blew the net curtains away from the open window. On the sill sat an open rosewood box.

But the glass was all over the floor.

XXXV

Whisky

The hour was late. He had been drinking. Not an unusual thing to do under the circumstances. Doubtless he was not the only one in the village troubled by the deaths, but they would keep to themselves, the townsfolk, the farmers. Huddled over ale and swapping theories. Rumours would abound about the grey man of Am Fear no doubt. Hard to shift legend in such a backwater.

He had little in common with them. They would come to him for medical reasons but beyond that they held him at arm's length. Two deaths, two murders, here in Lochnagar. What now walked the streets of this quiet village? A collector of blood and body parts. But for what purpose?

Abroad, he had seen so much that still haunted his dreams. Vile acts. Yet the removal of Hen's heart troubled him more. It spoke of ritual, of sacrifice. Yes, two murders, three, if one included the cat. Yes the cat, but vets did not write autopsy reports.

Perhaps he would pay the vet a visit, see if there was anything amiss. Yes the cat; there was a puzzle here to be solved. Tomorrow he would examine the thing if he was able. He would take James with him. Together they would piece this puzzle together… tomorrow.

With that he reached for the half-empty bottle of malt and poured himself another generous measure. He felt the whisky bite the back of his throat and closed his eyes. Leaning heavily back into his chair, he dozed, until an echo of guns of a Europe at war crept into the room. He clenched his eyelids, willing the memories of sound to disappear. For a brief moment they did and he sank back into the chair again, feeling the discomfort of the springs digging into his thighs. He had little desire to move and yet he should go to bed. What in God's name would tomorrow bring? The sound of something falling through the letterbox stirred him. What on earth would be posted at this late hour? The mail arrived early morning in the village, although he rarely received anything other than medical post. Those who would write letters and cards had all long gone.

*

One last task to perform. One last ingredient for a devil's recipe, the last token of a dybbuk's due. He stepped out into the street. The moonlight greeted him, casting a long shadow down the street. The shape pleased him. *Greatly.*

The surgery was before them, tall, semi-detached, two-storied, each with a pair of arched windows. A heavy door – battleship grey, stood below a pale yellow lamplight. A low privet and wooden gate guarded the property.

The cricket song of his castanet danced down the street as his final creation uncoiled itself from around his waist, wincing as the sharp claws dug into his flesh as it slowly crawled down his leg. Hesitating as it touched the ground, the centipede skittered gleefully across the street.

More than a metre of vertebrae attached to twenty pairs of segmented legs had been lovingly sculpted from rodent thigh bones, and fox, cat and lamb. Fused with intricate networks of piano wire, springs, cat gut, ligaments and tendons. Its fist-sized, heart-shaped head fashioned from overlapping layers of teeth. Clusters of silver pinhead circuitry formed its eyes. Fangs sat spring loaded, containing delicate syringes of puffer fish venom, concocted in those laboratories deep beneath the ruination of Berlin.

The centipede moved with a gentle undulation, sidewinder-like, across the cobbles. The synchronisation of so many limbs had been difficult to achieve, yet here it was; perfect fluid motion. So smooth, so quick, so deadly, perhaps his greatest creation yet. He allowed himself the intensity of pride.

As if reading their master's mind, the large shapes behind him began a slow, almost sad, covetous chatter, shifting their weight in their rustling robes. He silenced them with a series of clicks, dismissing them back to the shadows. Shadows, so easy to find on this street where the houses leant inwards, eager to witness this most perfect of deaths.

*

A drunken mariner's gait propelled Malcolm down his surgery's corridor. Yet another night spent in his chair with a single malt sedative. A mind devoid of memory, of a dream that was perhaps never there. The whiskey had his gratitude. Frequently.

Passing the doorway to the waiting room, he fumbled for the light switch at the base of the stairs. His mind was sluggish with indecision. A short climb up the stairs to a waiting bed held more appeal than a return to his office chair.

Curiosity won the battle over the need for rest, tinged with annoyance and he made his way down the corridor. Posters with the latest health advice were pinned to a large board just to the right of the front door. Unsteadily he paused at the mirror. Of late his eyes rarely met the bloodshot ones staring back at him. Instead he focused on his chin, running a hand over ever-greying stubble.

This village. The deaths, the night watchman, Major Evelyn. He had thought he had left death behind on the fields of Europe. But it had searched for him and found him in a sleepy village in the Highlands. What had this brave new world become?

He supposed officers would come from the larger towns until these crimes were solved. He fervently hoped sooner rather than waiting for the next. The people of Lochnaghar would need their doctor, if only to talk about their worries or fears.

Need him. Odd thought really. A better him. Perhaps he could do this, make himself right, make himself better. Physicians heal themselves it would appear. No one else could. Perhaps he could forget the pieces of himself he had left with the dead and the dying and find new pieces? To slot in. Replacements. Or not.

Wryly he shook his head, leaving the whimsy and the mirror. The letter-collecting basket had been replaced at some point in the dim and very distant past by a tin box with a hinged lid, secured with a flip catch. It was painted an oppressive dark grey. Malcolm had never liked it; it reminded him too much of helmets.

He flicked open the catch, lifted the lid and peered inside. He found neither envelope nor parcel but a coiled length of bone and claws. The sight shocked him, as a pair of tiny silver clustered eyes regarded him, a jaw yawned open exposing viper fangs. The creature shifted, letting out a slow hiss. Then it sprang.

He threw himself backwards, scrabbling away on his knees, not daring to take his eyes off the thing as it slowly snaked towards him. Desperately he tried to clear his head. He needed a weapon – any weapon. The creature suddenly lashed, grasping his forearm as more layers of teeth sprang from its upper jaw. He gripped it below the head with both hands.

There was no bravery in him now. Long since extinguished. Only panic and horror at the nightmare creature that pressed him into the floor, constricting itself around his neck. Frantically he struggled to find purchase on the writhing metal and bone creature that flinched, hissed, jabbed. Clutching the neck, Malcolm squeezed until his fingers latched together and he felt something inside of it shatter.

With a fluid motion he spun, tossing it towards the door. Fragments splintered, shards fell at his feet. The creature lay stilled for a second before it dragged itself into the mail box.

He needed to close the lid. Frantically he could think of nothing, found nothing. The mirror – he could hit it with the mirror or use it as a shield at least, perhaps the glass may break which he could then weaponise.

Rising, backing away, his eyes never leaving the now inert letter tin. Reaching for the wall, he turned, scuttling and scratching sounded from down the corridor. He looked, checking the floor, skirting boards, walls – nothing. He took the mirror from the wall.

The scuttling returned, gentler this time; he once again checked the same places – nothing. He relaxed slightly, hopefully it had returned from whence it came. The letter catcher was still open, its lid hanging limply.

He gripped the mirror tightly and began his approach. Step by step he drew closer. Poised ready to strike ,he lashed out a foot at the box. Nothing stirred. Inch by inch, weapon ready he peered inside. Empty. Slumping with relief, he placed the mirror at his feet and secured the box lid. Words began to form as his disbelieving mind tried to rationalise what had just happened. He picked up the mirror and turned. His eyes met the swaying open jaws dripping with toxins as the creature unfurled itself from the ceiling. A scream stolen in his throat as the creature's fangs clamped onto his mouth.

XXXVI

Broken things

The glazier arrived shortly after ten o'clock that morning to replace the glass. Duncan watched him closely. He was realising that things were changing around him, faster and faster. From now on he would keep an eye out for anything suspicious. He was worried about the special room in the outhouse though, filled with all his grandmother's silver and precious things. He hadn't told his mummy about it; it would make things worse. She would worry and he didn't want her to do any more of that. So he had played for quite a while in the other room. The pet that the man had given him skittered and romped, exploring the empty spaces and corners before returning to Duncan's hand.

The man who mended his window said to Mummy that it was most probably a bird that had flown into the window. A big one. Like an eagle? But the man had said no, most probably a large crow. There were lots in the nearby woods. It had probably been dazzled by the sun on the glass and flown into it. But there was no sign of it on the lawn below so it had probably just got a bruise on its beak and flown off.

When the glazier had gone and they were back to normal, he helped his mother bring down some things from the attic rooms and do a bit of exploring. Lovely things all hidden, Mummy had said. Two Lloyd Loom chairs and a matching footstool for the verandah. He thought Lloyd Loom was a funny name. Lots of ells's in it.

One of the chairs got stuck going round the edge of the landing, the bit where it turned sharply and he had to take a long breath because he thought he could have fallen, and if he broke his neck then there wouldn't be anyone to look after Mummy with all the bad things happening. Also the furniture was dusty and he had to stop himself from coughing.

She suggested he help her paint them, as the day was so lovely, so he did. And had a lovely time, he had to say. Took his mind off the things in the hidden room. White and several coats, and then when they were dry she said they would make some cushion covers for them so that they looked plump and welcoming. He asked her where they would put them and she said on the verandah outside the dining room would be just perfect. The canopy would keep them dry and they would bring them inside when it snowed.

221

One of them was a rocking chair and he thought he would have liked that in his bedroom. Sitting in it and swinging and playing with Buggy.

XXXVII

Walk

Duncan had begged her to let him walk to school on his own today. She wasn't sure he was old enough. The road could sometimes get busy. He looked a bit downhearted at this and said he was a big boy, nearly nine and he knew to walk tight up against the side of the road and listen carefully for tractors or cars. Eventually she gave in but said she would collect him. Did they have an agreement on that? They did.

She watched him disappear from view at the end of the drive, a determination in his step and his satchel bumping, heavy with books and his pencils and his lunch. He still looked so small, she thought, so young, but she realised she couldn't keep him young forever. He needed to know she trusted him to grow into the adult his father would have been proud of. But still…

High in the eaves where the servants would have slept, the roofs sloped sharply to the left. Dormer windows had been opened and she could see beyond the garden and the loch to the smoke from house hearths curling aimlessly into a day of no breeze. Cobwebs still hung in their multitudes from corners and crevices.

At the spot where the stairs formed a landing there was a long, low oak table. Its surface was covered with candlesticks but there was also a set of figurines posed at one end. The table looked lovely there, and she would purchase some candles from the grocer's as soon as she had need to go there again.

Portraits in matching velvet frames hung upon the walls on either side of the dark stairs and although darkened and sepiad, she thought there was a look of Gordon in several of them. Perhaps his great grandfather?

There were few records she knew of about the family, but possibly a local historian or old school registers or even a library may give her some background knowledge. It was important for Duncan, as it was after all his inheritance, his ancestry, and a long line leading to this point. She must make sure it continued.

In the very last room in the eaves she found boxes of books. She had spent so much time wondering where to put all the furniture that she hadn't really looked into the boxes and trunks that were stacked there. Some were so dated she knew she would never read them, but there were a few about the area, which caught her attention. One in particular was simply titled *The Grey Men*. The cover was a bit grim. A tall hair-covered creature rearing its head above the standing stones.

Evidence of this creature is limited to various sightings and a few photographs of unusual footprints... an extremely tall figure covered with short hair, or as an unseen presence that causes uneasy feelings in people who climb the mountains. Some believe that Am Fear Liath Mòr is a supernatural being, possibly a wild "Greyman" of Scottish folklore, roams the mountains in search of food. Ripping the throats of sheep and goats.

A lone climber – Cooper – described terrifying noises near the summit of Ben MacDhui in the early 1920s. "I heard something else behind me. Every few steps I took, I heard a crunching upon the trail. I turned on several occasions but the mist had descended swiftly and I could barely make out the trail."Staggering blindly amongst the boulders and bracken he found the path to the village of Lochnagar and there reported his story to the local publican and other acquaintances.

Well, hopefully these creatures have found other mountains to roam, she thought. Wouldn't want the guests being frightened out their wits! She had become so absorbed in the book, sitting in the front parlour, the sun streaming through windows still patterned from the ivy she had removed, that she was startled when the clock on the bookcase chimed. Duncan. He would be waiting for her at school. She had never been late before. Hurrying down the road to collect her child, she wondered if she looked like the wild man from the corries.

Children wandered or ran down the lane in various directions to homes and farms, the call of late tea beckoning hungry stomachs. The air was full of their laughter and callings. Waiting at the entrance to the small schoolhouse she searched the clusters for her child. There was a pause in the line exiting the school and the master appeared on the steps, smiled at her in greeting. "He's a bright laddy your wee son. He's a love of history." She nodded and asked if she could help in any way at home. Help him to catch up on lessons he had missed. Delightful idea he replied and bidding her good afternoon, went back inside the building.

She waited for another few minutes, but no more children left the school, and the trailing sounds of the children had long gone. Concerned, she finally knocked on the door. After a pause the teacher opened it and looked at her with a curious expression. Duncan had left with the others, he replied, some twenty minutes ago. Home he presumed?

*

The water had remained as it was when they had visited for the first time. At the summit he could see the reflection of the late sky upon it, rippling in a wind he couldn't feel. And the stones, standing heavy. Was it deep? He didn't think he wanted to find out. The big boys were braver and waded in calling for him to do the same, but Mummy would know where he'd been if he came back very wet, and she would be sad and disappointed.

But he had so wanted to see what was in the deep hole, beneath the very tallest of the stones. This time he thought the stone looked unkind. Stern, a blade of grey shearing the sky.

Like a man.

It had water in it when he peered over the edge, slightly afraid of its depth. Now he wouldn't know if there were skeletons in it or not. The big boys had said that this was where they threw the bodies of the sacrifices hundreds of years ago. Maybe longer. And they were still there because no one was brave enough to go in there and find them. He had wanted to ask why they were sacrificed, but hesitated in case they thought he was stupid.

It was getting a bit too late now and a sudden mist caught him by surprise. He could just see the big boys, although they had disappeared down the avenue of the little stones that he had thought looked like gnomes. He thought he had better go home now and started to walk in the direction of the little gate in the low hedge. Behind him he heard the big boys calling to him. Mockingly they asked him why he was running away. He said he wanted to go home because it was late and his mummy would be worried. Mummy? Only babies say that word, came the echo as the mist grew thicker and he could only hear their words through a muffle of the cloud. Was he scared of the ghosts up here? No, he said, although inside he thought he was.

Above him he saw red in the sky that seemed to be hurrying away from this place just as he wanted to. The sky was older and braver than he was. The big boys were braver than he was. He should be braver because he had to look after Mummy now that Daddy was gone. The man of the house she had called him and that had made him proud.

But not brave.

In front of him the mist hadn't yet obscured the corrie. It was wrinkled as though frowning in disapproval at his lack of courage. Deep veins in the rock where the earth had retched and thrown it up, lines like the old man had on his face. Very deep, farm furrows. He was very old. Duncan was sure that he too was a brave man. He had done lots of things in his life. The old man had said he had travelled to so many lands he had forgotten just how many. Duncan had asked if he had seen the pyramids and the old man had nodded and said yes.

Perhaps when he was a big boy and brave he would take Mummy and they would ride in a barge down the Nile, which was the longest river in the world. Or was that the Amazon? He could never remember.

Recalling the old man, he made a decision to go home. He would ask him about the sacrifices. He didn't say anything to the big boys but hurried through the gate and down the small hill that led into the village. They would be unkind tomorrow he was sure. Big boys always were, but he wanted to be in the warm kitchen, with the smell of bread and food, with his mummy and the old man.

*

Frantically Annette searched around the school building; the teacher behind her soothingly saying that he was sure

Duncan had gone home on his own, their paths must have crossed. Surely. Her head was in a whirl and the panic that had started as a worry was growing inside her heart. The "what ifs" gathered pace and she failed to stop them. Round and round they went as she ran up the lane and down their path towards the house. All was dark inside, even though it was high afternoon with the mists on the ground and hills.

Calling his name, she fruitlessly looked in each room and the outhouses that he seemed drawn to. Without a telephone she was isolated, torn between going back to the village or staying here to wait for him, she knew she should be calm. She knew she had to think practically. But the "what ifs" gathered and gathered until all she could see was emptiness as the dusk settled.

She forced herself to breathe slowly and calmly, pressing her hand to her chest to feel the heart slow its frantic pace. A note. Leave him a note on the kitchen table. It would be the first place he sought her when he returned. Hurriedly she told him to stay at home, that she would be back.

The only place she thought he might have gone would be Dolly's. Up one of the narrow lanes that led from the main square. To spend some time with Bertie? Perhaps the boys were playing in the garden, thinking nothing of the fact she had no knowledge of where he was. In a child's world such worries evaporated.

Passing the police station she hesitated briefly, a shard of further anxiety within her. She would check with Dolly, do that first. Perhaps it wouldn't come to reporting him missing, but deep inside there was always that fear. She wasn't stoic like her mother. She wasn't brave. She was a mouse. A clockwork mouse. Small and timid. And her world was splintering second on second as she knocked with her fists on the doors.

The darkening happened so swiftly she had no idea when it began. So many roads she had searched, and called. People came out of doors or looked through windows and all she could hear was blurrings of words and faces, so many faces, as images flooded her and she found it hard to breathe or think. Like rapid bullets they came. So rapid and rapid and her chest ached and her legs that felt wooden refused to stop. Such thoughts and she called his name over and over. And over, as she ran back through the village leaving farmers, and wives, and shopkeepers staring at her, whispering worries, coats over nightwear.

Whispering worries.

Dragging the door to the house open, she screamed now into the emptiness that seemed to always be there. Even with dustings and clearings and the old man and her child. Still so very empty. His name hurtled to the attics with their frozen memories of a woman she had never met, who had died so quietly and lay days after her death.

Hurtled to the kitchen and the gardens that she knew she would never plant now. To the hill and the barren barn that no one owned, to the outhouses with their coal and their dust that had made his knees smile.

And a voice replied,

"Hello Mummy."

XXXVIII

Lurchings

The telephone broke through his sleep. James' hand snaked out from under the covers fumbling for the receiver. Still with one foot in the land of dreams, he placed the receiver to his ear. He was met with a loud hiss of static and the slow lurching sound of a low voice that resembled a gramophone being played backwards.

Then silence.

Cursing loudly he set the receiver back in place. Gathering the covers around him, he turned his back to the phone and shut his eyes. Scant seconds later the telephone once again rang. For a moment he thought about not answering it, but the burden of duty won the battle with his conscience and he picked up the receiver.

Once again his ear was bombarded with a wave of static, but this time there was a voice, a tiny, childlike voice. "Help him, mister, help him. Brown's field. He's hurting. Help him." With that came the hiss of static, and the phone being replaced.

He took a moment to gather himself. He lay on his back and struggled with the decision a moment, looking longingly at the empty space in his double bed, he patted the sheet where another once slumbered. "I know what you would have said, my dear," he whispered and swung his legs off the bed.

Dressing swiftly, he started the car, driving through the streets of the village. Within minutes he pulled the car up to the gate beyond which lay Brown's field. A shaky wooden barrier was flanked either side by chest-high dry stonewalling. He switched off the engine but left the lights on, their beams sweeping into the field. His watch told him it was nearly three o'clock. Stepping out of the car, he didn't bother shutting the door and leant over the gate.

The moon was large, not quite full, only the odd anaemic cloud drifted across the blackness. A million diamond pinpricks pierced the darkness and added to the moon's silver-grey gaze. He could see a good way into the field, almost all the way up to the heavy copse, perhaps the size of a small house. A dense tangle of tree and thicket where the crows slept. An island of twisted shadows surrounded by a sea of pewter grass blades.

The field's dimensions reminded the officer of a rough pentagon. It was a decent size, must have been twenty acres, walled on all sides, the narrow point of it at the apex of a steepish hill. Thick woods neighboured the upper walls, casting long shadows. Well, he was here now, may as well get on with it. He climbed the gate and switched on his torch to scan the grass around him.

Nothing. So.

He began the gentle climb to the crest of the hill, scanning with his torch this way and that. Still nothing. Rustles reached his ears, in the grass on either side of him, the hedgerows, trees, matching his every stride. He stopped. The noise did too, and as he moved so did the sound. Field mice perhaps, maybe a mole.

Twenty yards from the copse he saw the shadow. Hunched over, black, a man bending, child perhaps, but so vague as to be almost a thought, slipping from the clutch of trees just as his torch beam caught it. Startled, it sped off back into the darkness of the fields.

It wobbled with a curious gait like a child on stilts; smashing through branches and stumbling over roots deep into the copse until it was lost from sight. A child on stilts?

What stupid game was this? Taking his whistle from a breast pocket he gave three shrill blasts. He waited for movement but none came.

He noticed that crows had not taken flight at the sound. Only the sheep seemed to respond, small shapes of vague grey cotton squashed up in the "point" of the field, as far as it was physically possible to be from the spot where he now stood. He heard them blather. They were unsettled, herding together. Wrapping the cord of his whistle around his wrist, he took a deep breath and strode towards the trees.

The trail was easy enough to follow by torchlight so he picked his way carefully over roots, ducking branches. He glimpsed the shadow just up ahead, it seemed to stumble and fall. Soon he was upon it. Tackled, it lay there in a heap of black cloth. Inert. As he reached to unmask the person, a sudden movement behind him made him turn abruptly.

A second outline darkly loomed above him, and then took a sideways step.

"You!" James bellowed, rising to his feet. "Identify yourself." The shadow retreated into the depth of the copse, its only response to James' anger a series of repetitive wooden clicks. Hairs pricked up on the back of James' neck as he heard them and behind him he sensed the bundle of cloth rise with a gentle rustle of fabric. Torn between both trespassers, a tiny ember of fear took root in the policeman's heart.

It rose, stiff and unnatural, to its full height. Taller than he by a full head or more. It stood stock-still, hooded head bowed, clad in a long robe, black, matt, Druid-like. Over-long sleeves hanging limply by its sides, it lurched into life.

"Stay put, you bastard," James shouted trying to glimpse the face beneath the hood. His hand held up, palm out – signalling a halt. The robe spasmed forward, awkward, legs stiff, stilt-like, movements orchestrated now in time to the deafening clicking from the copse. It halted at his open palm, head remaining bowed, pressing against the flesh of his hand. His touch did not bring an image of flesh and blood beneath the robe as to his horror he realised his fingers were pressed against bones, ribs. Panic filled him as the thing in front of him twitched, but James was faster.

In a heartbeat his hand was through the leather loop of his truncheon, the weapon grasped. Adrenalin surged. Time to fight. "Right, bastard," he roared, "let's deal with this Glasgae style," and swung with all his might.

The weapon struck the cowled head with a loud crack, he felt the impact resonate up to his shoulder, the very bones of his arm aching in reply as the hooded head snapped sideways with a sickening sound.

Something had broken.

The head slowly turned with a whirr of a mechanism, the hood and veil falling away revealing the nightmare visage beneath. The skull of a ram regarded him with blank sockets above a lower jaw dislodged to one side, barely suspended by thin wires whose small screws were buried deep in yellowing bone. James took a step back as revulsion surged through him, his mind barely believing the image.

His soul screamed in horror, heart racing in panic as his mouth filled with ash.

"Dear God," was all his trembling lips could whisper.

"No God here policeman," came the voice from the darkness. It was old, ancient, Germanic.

The creature lunged with an arm that ended not with a hand but with two sheep jaws wired together in a perversion of a crab-like claw. Backing away James was trapped against the trunk of a tree. Halting his escape.

Too late. It was now too late.

He raised his torch hand to defend himself as the creature arced its claw to clamp his forearm, ruminant teeth pierced his skin and like a macabre crane, the creature lifted James off his feet.

Roaring in pain he struck the limb of the figure once, then twice, until it buckled but held him fast nonetheless. With a sickening grinding of gears, it twisted about its axis and hurled him back against the tree like a discarded rag doll. Winded, he slid to the ground, gasping as his ribs splintered.

He tried to rise as the creature lurched forward. Once again the crab claw grabbed his wrist, teeth biting deep, blood now flowed freely down his arm. He roared in pain as it hauled him to his knees. He grunted as it bent his arm backwards, twisting him to kneel in front of it. A further pull and it was behind him, holding him tight, an almost half-nelson. Cloth tore and pain erupted inside him, there was a sickening wet tearing sound, his eyes bulged in pain and terror as with agonising slowness a spike of sculptured bone tore through his arching back and the cloth of his uniform and appeared from his abdomen.

The pain was unbearable, but it had not killed him. Screaming in pain, rage and horror. Someone would come, someone would hear him. He would be rescued. In his mind's eye he saw the shade of his wife urging him to fight. Blinking away the tears – Fight James!

Fight!

XXXIX

And then

Afternoon was slowly dissolving into memory as the Clockmaker entered the house. Lochnagar had been a hive of nervous activity – not surprising considering recent events. So he moved slowly, quietly, going about the business in hand. Sliding between the minutes and the hours.

Click click.

The hallway rose to greet him with the appetising aroma of steamed trout and boiled vegetables. One last meal, that was all that was left of this long, long journey over decades, centuries. He was tired.

The atmosphere in the kitchen was palpable. Duncan sat bent over his tea pushing vegetables around with a fork.

His mother, her back to him, busied herself with an over-exaggerated display of checking the potatoes. He paused at the door and said, "Hello", Annette turned and smiled weakly. Dressed in pale blue, her housecoat gathered at the waist by a white pinafore, which showed how thin she was. She looked pale, bloodshot eyes, which spoke of many tears recently shed. Her shoulders were high and tense.

Duncan didn't acknowledge the old man's presence; he continued to push cauliflower round his plate with a fork, most of the meal untouched. Annette saw the old man's hesitation and good manners getting the better of her, she indicated he take his seat at the table.

As he sat on Duncan's right, the boy lifted his head. His pale complexion matched that of his mother, his eyes dark and sunken. Finally he asked, "Is there anything I may help you with?"

Annette shook her head and said it was a family matter that they had resolved.

XL

Gone

His tormentor stood stock still as if unsure what to do, puzzled at the lack of his victim's demise. The wound had not killed him. He looked down at the bone that had pierced his body. His lips trembled as his mind raced for a solution. With a shaking hand, he grasped the bone and gripped it tight. He screamed at the top of his lungs, pain stabbed at every atom of his being and he braced himself and pushed. A small part of the spike disappeared inside him. It was agony but he would escape this and burn this bastard straight to hell.

Panting hard he pushed again, blood welled and pain flared but a small progress rewarded him. The wound might not kill him but bleeding to death would. Perhaps that was the monster's plan all along. Well, not today. James Hendry would not breathe his last like some slaughtered lamb.

Screaming at the top of his lungs, blinking away the pain with streaming eyes, with gritted teeth he began to push himself to freedom inch by excruciating inch. He did not hear the wooden clicks behind him. He did not hear the rustle of undergrowth leaf litter. He did not see the tiny constructs of stolen bone, wire and spinning cog approach. His eyes wide, he finally saw them as they reached his knees.

Ignoring the pain, the torment, he swept down with his arm scattering them. All but one – a small, fist-sized ladybird, sculptured teeth and rat bones. It leapt up his chest. Pain and loss of blood slowed him as it climbed up his body, tiny claws digging into his neck flesh, releasing small peals of blood. With a twitch of legs it jumped onto his face and dug its forelegs into his lips as he clenched his teeth.

Tiny legs tried in vain to prise open his clammed-up lips. Finally the monster behind him moved. It raised its arm that ended in the impaling spike just a fraction, as if it did not have the strength in that arm to lift James' body. James roared in fury as fire lanced through him. It was all the little beast needed as it pushed its way into his mouth on probing legs, instantly gagging the victim.

James retched. He tried to vomit, but the creature dug deep into buccal flesh and moved even further. His eyes bulged as fire in his throat told him the invader had begun to chew. He clamped down with his jaws and ground with all his might. Teeth broke, more pain flared but he felt something inside his jaws snap, the creature lost its footing slightly and he spat out a blob of blood, tooth fragment and legs of bone.

Fury overtook him and power surged through him, fuelled by horror and pain, so much pain. His jaws clamped tight, pinning the creature fast, lungs burning in protest.

Clutching the bone spike he pushed with what little strength remained. The spike disappeared inside, yet he was still pinned. Hope rose. Dear God, he was going to do this. The euphoria lasted for a brief moment.

For.

Stumbling through the trees came the second monstrous construct; robes flapping freely exposing ribs of cattle, innards of cogs and wire. The skull of a horse looked down at him with empty eyes. He slumped in defeat as he saw its exposed arm. A bovine femur pinned to the shoulder, a cog of an elbow connected a human thighbone to a blade hand carved into the shape of a scythe.

As the blood mist clouded him, a spike of sculptured bone tore through his arching back, scything in a final arc of victory for the cowled construct. As blood vomited through his screaming lips he saw the shade of his wife screaming at him to fight.

I can't my dear. I can't.

And so he did not hear the wooden clicks behind him. He did not hear the rustle of undergrowth leaf litter. He did not see the tiny constructs of stolen bone, wire and spinning cogs approach. They reached his knees. Ignoring the pain, the torment he swept down with his arm scattering them. All but one. A small fist-sized ladybird, all sculptured teeth and rat bones, that leapt upon his chest. It clambered upwards – tiny claws digging into his neck flesh, releasing small peals of blood.

As the creature burrowed and chewed and the vast blackness with the sockets of the horse skull lowered, all his yesterdays rushed – a child in shorts running in the yard with a toy wooden plane. Parents straight and beaming as he took his badge of office. Two graves on a cold and rainy autumn morn. His wife's smiling face looking up at him in a bright summer's meadow.

Ah my love, he sighed.

The wires twitched, an elbow cog turned, the scythe fell and P.C. James Hendry's head flew from his shoulders, screaming through a shower of red.

XLI

Dishes

Dishes. There were always dishes to be cleaned. A small boy and their guest of course. She had become used to having him here. She wondered where he would go when he left them. Annette thought about leaving the washing-up, but she would just have to do it in the morning anyway and she didn't like the idea of leaving a sink full of dirty dishes overnight. She worried that if she did, she may slip into bad habits. And it would only take a few minutes.

Soon there would be many guests who would lodge here during the walking months. When the weather was warm and they would head out of a morning with satchels full of luncheons. By then she would have help.

A young lass from the village, perhaps a lad to help with the garden.

A half-boiled kettle would be enough for a few plates and cups. She had forgotten to get rubber gloves again. Her hands had become dry and chapped and really quite unsightly despite the fact she lathered them with Pond's night cream at bedtime. Ah well.

Washing the plates with a dishcloth, her mind turned to the murdered man. What a dreadful, dreadful thing to happen. Poor man. Attacked by animals it was rumoured. She would have to make sure Duncan was extra careful when playing outside from now on.

She had liked his calmness and strength in times of distress. She only hoped he hadn't suffered at the end. In truth she would miss the friendship they were forming. She felt her throat tighten and thought she might cry again. Gripping the edge of the sink she had stern words with herself. Drying her hand on her apron, she brushed a stray strand of hair from her forehead and breathed deeply. Oh for goodness' sake, she was becoming maudlin. Stacking the plates on the dresser, she then hung up her apron and wiped the surface of the kitchen table, wondering what conversations were held in this very room between those long gone.

All was quiet and still. Stepping out into the back, she listened to the sounds of the night. An owl and a fox. Nocturnal company. Punctuating the late hour with their calls to others, she presumed. No doubt the old man would be able to explain why those in the wild called.

A sound that was not of the wild disturbed her thoughts.

A click.

From within. Then another. Smiling, she knew that someone had come downstairs into the kitchen. A nice warm drink.

There was no one inside so she assumed either Duncan or the old man had gone back upstairs. She'd boil the water anyway. She reached for the kettle to fill it. Tea or cocoa. Something that wouldn't keep them awake, milky. If she had looked up in that instant she would have seen the shadow pass before the glass.

But she didn't, did she?

"Would you like a warm drink before bed?" she asked, as she heard the man enter the kitchen, the clicking of his walking stick and a now familiar dragging of his leg and feet. She glanced up at the window's reflection to smile at him and dropped the kettle.

Behind her reared a raven black figure far taller than she. She spun on her heel as a scream fought its way through her and she found her eyes level with a rib cage of yellowed bone, cogs and wires that clicked and spun, and she moved her gaze upwards as the screaming found its way.

Empty sockets in a skull of a chattering ram. Their gaze from beneath a ragged hood pinned her in terror as the creature's claw whipped in a brief, clipped arc and she crashed against the cold, cold stone of the sink. Heavily. Crumpling to the tiles the warm liquid began to pool around her temple. Words spoken from far away reached her.

"This you do not deserve... of all the people... however... I am not going to help you."

Her eyes flickered open, small flashing sparks flew in front of her and she couldn't feel or move her arms. She found herself inches away from a pair of hooves beneath a soiled hem. With a moan she tried to raise her head, to pull away, to hide. And with the name of her child on her lips she did not feel the final blow that brought her darkness.

XLII

Shine

The dreamer once again soared with the Spitfires in skies of crystal ocean blue, sitting in the cockpit of a Lancaster alongside his co-pilot, Roy Miller, dressed splendidly in fur-lined leather. The interior was shiny and new, with dials and clocks that ticked away on the dashboard. The man was kind and smiled at him, telling him he was the best pilot he had ever flown with.

Flying through the sky, Spitfires buzzed around them, looped the loop as the navigator made a pot of tea and sliced an enormous Battenberg.

Far, far below the little red train ran on tracks of mercury silver. The hills had gone to be replaced by level green monotone.

Tonight the little fairy had returned. But not as Duncan had ever seen him before. This time the dybbuk was a little ball of neon-blue candle flame; hovering just over the front of the train. No smoke rose from its funnel; it ran clean.

When the shadows of the monsters came, visible just out of the corner of the eye, the little blue flame would dance away and chase them off. Spitfires would turn and strafe, machine guns spitting. The monsters would shrink and hide and the flame would float back to the front of the train. The warplanes returned and gave spiralling chase to Duncan's gleaming Lancaster bomber. Buggy nestled closer and sang his soothing song of clicks and chimes and the monsters were easily lost in a feast of tea and cake.

*

Hours passed and the moon rose high. Duncan's room was bathed in silver, window firmly shut. The young boy slept soundly, knowing he was safe and sound, watched over, loved. But Buggy became restless, shifting from beneath the pillow, scuttling out through the door.

*

The monsters had returned, long shadows terrifying and looming; impossible giants, scattering the train and the beautiful silver rails. A thousand eyes and teeth like tigers, the feet of birds. They spied the warplanes and chased after them, swatting at them with their massive claws. One Spitfire down, then another. They reached out for the doomed bomber and Duncan's eyes snapped open.

*

He sat up in his bed and waited for wakening; his heart began to slow as the images of the shadow monsters melted from his mind. Tucking his hand beneath his pillow he reached for the comfort of Buggy, but Buggy was nowhere to be found. Hearing noises in the corridor he went to find his pet.

There was a long carpet that stretched all the way from one end of the corridor to the other. It didn't go around the corners though, because carpets can't. Mummy had said it was a Persian carpet. You could tell because of the rich silk colours – red and amber and ochre. Big words for colours. She had told him artists used those words to describe paints.

Along the corridor he could see the old man's door slightly open, light filtering out through the gap. He crept past his mother's room, not wanting to wake her.

A few steps away from the guest room his weight shifted a loose floorboard. The noises in the room paused, the activity of rustles, clicks and scrapings. The old man appeared at his door. Duncan froze, feeling guilty. He wasn't quite sure why. It was his house after all.

The old man just smiled, a finger to his lips, beckoning Duncan into the room. An oil lamp sat on the floor and Duncan thought this was silly. What would happen if it fell over? The house could burn down and then where would they live?

The old man was wearing his day clothes, heavy boots on his feet. His coat was laid out on his bed. "Couldn't sleep?"

Duncan shook his head. "I lost Buggy, he ran off."

"They do that sometimes. He'll come back soon," the old man said soothingly.

"Are you leaving?" Duncan asked, eyeing the coat on the bed. He thought it a bit odd that the bed was so neatly made. His wasn't. Perhaps that's what grown-ups did. Made their bed in the middle of the night. He would have to ask Bertie about this.

"I thought I might go for a look around."

"For the monsters?"

The old man let out a little chuckle. "There are no monsters my dear, just dream beings. But perhaps I cast a glance, just the same?"

"I think I should come too. Because of Mummy and this house."

The old man crossed his arms and shook his head. "Ah no, it is late. You are young. Your mother would be worried and disapproving of me."

"But we won't tell her, she'll never know as long as we are back before breakfast. Oh please, I promise I won't tell, it'll be our secret, I didn't tell about Buggy. Please?"

"Our little secret?"

"Promise?"

"Dress quickly, and we will be silent. Yes?"

With that the boy disappeared from the room.

He returned to find the man sitting on his bed, waiting patiently. Duncan was dressed in his long trousers that he should only wear for church, a white shirt half-stuffed into the waistband, a red woollen cardigan, and his winter coat.

"I think we shall take some company, boy. What do you think?" Puzzled, Duncan watched as he pulled the castanet from his pocket and opened the wardrobe door. The mirror saw Duncan. He would like a wardrobe with a mirror on it. He would ask Mummy.

Tomorrow. After the old man and he had made sure the monsters weren't real.

Tiny clicking shards of light formed, and the gloom of the wardrobe coalesced into miniscule shapes and forms. Another click and a small avalanche of bone creatures poured out onto the floor, mechanisms oiled, claws scraping. Dozens it seemed.

Scattering in their release, Duncan gazed in amazement. "My beauties. My constructs..." the old man breathed. "What do you think to them? Are they not true beauty? You have nothing to fear, they won't hurt you."

Part of the boy was scared and wanted to run, part of him wanted to stay, to see and wonder. Somehow the old man had an air about him, a comfort in his words and his presence.

They were forming a circle around the man. Ladybirds and mice, scorpions and rodents, their brass keys turning slowly above spines of leg bones, tails that arched above their backs quivering with stinging points, poised to strike. Outstretched pincers made from rodent skulls clicking in time with every other construct around him.

Finally, there emerged from the wardrobe a full rat skeleton, innards replaced with clicking cogs of brass and steel, organs thin tubes of glass that glowed with unsettling pale blues and greens, the bones held together with needle-thin wires and intricate ropes that appeared to be woven from human hair, its movement flawless.

The Clockmaker smiled down at them, spreading his hands like a conjuror, enjoying the young boy's wonder at the creatures he had made. He frowned and rubbed his cheek. He checked his wrist-watch, turned to Duncan and said, "It is time we must leave."

The old man collected an army kit bag from the bottom of the wardrobe, placing it on the floor. The constructs all began to file towards it and one by one they slithered in through the opening in the top. Duncan felt something nudge his foot. He looked down to see Buggy sitting there, its tail end quivering like an excited puppy.

"There, he has come back to you, young man." Duncan smiled with glee and cupped the creature in his hands and gazed at it lovingly.

"Put him in your pocket, he'll be warm there." Duncan gently rolled Buggy into his coat pocket. The old man took a cage device from the table next to the bed and slid the bundle into the kit bag, shuffling the constructs around to make space for it. Satisfied, he gently lifted the bag until it sat on its end. Gathering up the bag, he stooped down. "Ready?"

The boy looked into the man's eyes. They were so pale. Like loch water. Flat and grey. "You're a special boy, you do know that?" Duncan smiled, held captive by this wonderful man who could create such incredible creatures.

"Would you care to carry something exceptional?" Duncan smiled. The old man reached under his pillow and produced the small rosewood box. Duncan's eyes widened as he saw it. The old man smiled wryly and handed it to him. It felt different this time, heavier somehow, warm. "A good luck charm, my dear." The boy nodded, accepting the man's words and placed it in his empty coat pocket.

They crept out of the room together and quietly slipped out of the house.

XLIII

Oblivion

Oblivion is easy. There is no pain, no hurt, no struggle nor hardship. No love, no joy, no passion. In the war, men lay down and died rather than continue the hell of their struggle. Had they been tales, nothing more? To shame those accused of cowardice. White feathers fluttered around her. Soft. And snow-like. Why was it snowing she wondered?

Did the men who landed on the Normandy beaches choose oblivion? Did the men above the skies of Britain when the Luftwaffe came in their droves? Did Walter, at El Alamein, at Tobruk, living in a hole in the ground in the desert? No, he did not. Why?

Because of love, of joy, of life.

Because of Nora and Anne and the countless others who waited for him, needed him to fight, to struggle, to take the hurt for them. And when oblivion came and offered its dark embrace, they got back up... cut and bleeding. They got up, took another step forward and raged against its promise to take all the pain away. Like Walter, like Gordon had, like she knew he had at the end.

Oh Gordon.

"Take my hand Annette." A gentle whisper in the dark. The feathers still falling and falling upon her face. Like strokings they were. She tried to reach for them, for the hand but it fell through her fingers like smoke.

"Get up sweetheart, get up."

Reaching again towards the voice with a hand she could not see. Knowing the voice with such longing. But darkness was everything. And she loved the quietness. Much quieter than anything she had felt before. The kind of no noise before the world found its feet and stood up.

She knew then that she was dying.

XLIV

Rapture

Duncan watched in rapt awe as the rippling blues and greens slowly approached from the North. He sat with the old man on the stone altar, legs swinging as he enjoyed the moment.

The man's strange clock sat next to them, the crystal at its apex giving off a faint glow. They had not found any monsters yet but the old man had promised him that tonight was a very special night. That the Northern Lights would soon be right above the very spot on which they sat.

"Where do they come from?" and the old man told him of sunspots and charged particles in the air. "Like electricity?" the boy had asked. "Yes just that," the old man had confirmed. Satisfied with the explanation Duncan had leant his head heavily on the Clockmaker's arm, just to close his eyes for a minute while they waited.

Duncan awoke to the old man's whisper. He felt the man's fingers smoothing his hair. As he shook the sleep from himself, he felt the man's arm around his shoulder. Duncan didn't really mind. The old man was his friend.

His surroundings registered and he jumped off the stone altar. Hands in front of him, he turned them this way and that as the yellow and green light bathed his skin. Head tilted, he gazed at the sky around him. The old man had been as good as his word.

Above them hung the Aurora Borealis. Sparkling greens, blues and yellows danced above them and bathed them in such wondrous light, like coral at the bottom of a sparkling sea. Duncan looked at his hands and fingers turning them this way and that as they changed with the colour swirling above them. Lights so low he felt he could reach up and touch them. Almost, the old man had said, brought close to earth by a little bit of science, a little bit of nature and touch of magic. Their very own magic circle.

Forks of pink lightning born in the curtain above, split the darkness beyond them with a loud crack. Another, then another. Duncan found himself clinging to the old man as it struck the same spot in the grass, over and over. Pink coruscating worms of energy writhed away from the point of impact, singeing the grass at their passing, until evaporating into darkness.

A twin bolt struck another point in the dark. Duncan clamped his hands over his ears against the deafening whip cracks. He buried his head against the old man as fluorescent lightning stained his sight. All around him seemed to be noise and light, strobing the hillside, lashing together corrie and sky until he curled himself up tightly and prayed it would end.

As quickly as it had started, the lightening ceased. Duncan's ears still rang with its call. Uncurling himself after endless seconds he stared up at the old man. The old man looked down at him with sadness.

"What is happening? Is it a hurricane?" The old man pointed to the altar, the crystal at the top of his clock glowing strongly now as the machine's armatures spun wildly, illuminating the stone plinth in its light. His gaze returned to the puzzled young boy.

"It is time, now… your time." Duncan looked up at him in confusion.

"Look." The old man pointed, Duncan turned to the spot where the lightning had struck. Amongst the smouldering grass, two shapes began to rise. They grew out of the darkness, giants robed in black. The old man placed his hand on Duncan's quivering shoulders.

"*The monsters, they come.*"

XLV

Smear

Her eyes were so very heavy, lids gummed shut, her head throbbing. "Get up, Annette." The voice was calm, gentle; there was command but such love laced within its words.

There had always been so much love.

Oblivion shivered and shrank away as she dragged her eyes open. And saw. Saw in the doorway, framed by light, a tall silhouette, broad of shoulder, narrow of hip. Uniformed – an airman's cap.

"Get up Annette, our child needs you…" Light faded. Oblivion made its final plea to take away the pain. She rebuffed its promises. *Duncan needs me. He does.* Through the pain she raised her head, but the doorway was empty.

There are few things in the universe that compare to the strength of the bond between a mother and her child. Love is too small a word. To this particular mother it was a chain of steel, forged in the hearth of birth pain, tempered in the fires of the loss of a father, a companion, a soul mate, a one true love.

Had Gordon felt the pull of that chain too? Had he stood in the doorway? Had he called her from the void of unconsciousness to deliver her the warning? Or was it just a trick of the mind.

Oh Gordon I know it was you.

Annette rose on unsteady legs. With shaking fingers she gingerly touched the wound; it was tender to the touch, protruding from her temple, crusted over in dry blood. It was all she could do not to cry out. Her head thundered and her ears rang. As she focused she saw she had pulled herself up by using shelves as support. Why was she in the pantry? A trail of blood along the floor into the kitchen spoke of her journey dragged across the floor and hidden from sight.

Time began to catch up with her, drawing back the shade of unconsciousness. What had attacked her? Images of bones, a ram skull leering out from under a hood, a rib cage under which she saw hints of spinning cogs of tubes and wires. Hooves bolted to long bones that served as legs. It was no ghost, goblin or spectre. A ghastly aberration, the product of human artifice.

But who and why? The old man! He was there! It was with him. Duncan…

Adrenalin surged as shock sprung her into action. One foot in front of the other, her legs reluctantly obeying her, she swayed her way through the kitchen, from cabinet to table to doorway, a drunkard's progress that steadily sobered with each footfall.

Her journey from the pantry to the staircase was a migraine smear of sharp furniture edges and hard walls. Of hands and knees hitting carpet. The panicked scratching of fingers as she clawed herself to her feet. A drowning sailor scrambling for the surface for a breath of air.

For Duncan.

She knew she should not be standing. She knew she should still be lying on the floor in the pantry, unmoving, her mind locked from her body, boxed away from whatever was happening around her, from whatever was happening to her Duncan. Perhaps her assailant had concluded the same and decided to stay its hand, perhaps it just thought she was dead or soon would be. *Gordon did you...?*

Reaching the stairs, her boy's name a constant scream. Treads missed, falls and bruised knees, hands and elbows, she stumbled into his room. An empty bed and small pajamas heaped on the floor. A mother's nightmare made reality. No time. She span on her heel and stumbled down the corridor to the old man's room.

Gone. Empty.

Wardrobe door flung open, devoid of contents. Fear, pain and rage erupted from her core. A raging volcano of pure hatred burst from within her that she had never known she was capable of. A mother wronged, a child taken with the intent to do harm from a man who made monsters. A man they had taken pity on; had welcomed into her home, into her family and in some small way their hearts. The hurt, the betrayal! He had taken her one and only, her first and last born.

Fire surged through her veins, burning adrenalin pumped through her limbs and with all her might Annette ran.

Ran.

XLVI

Run!

Somewhere inside her, her body screamed for her to stop. To stop running. But the grief within her would not dim nor grow passive. It raged against the oblivion call. It hurled her onward. It screamed her son's name between each painful gasp of air. Screams that echoed along the streets of a slumbering Lochnagar.

As she dragged herself down the streets, she could see house lights wink on. She called out to God, to Gordon, desperate promises passed her lips, she would do anything, anything, to save her child. Two burly shadows rushed towards her.

And screaming, she fell.

Flaring pain prised open her eyes. Bright lights. Too bright. Her head swam as she blinked away the fog to focus on the stranger looking down at her. Sympathetic pale blue eyes. Some stranger who said she was Mary.

Struggling to focus her eyes, a well-worn white dressing gown hastily tied over a long nightdress of faded pink blurred before her, and the blood. A bloodied wet cloth. Annette threw her head backwards, pulling away from the blood and the pain that slewed through her.

"Hush, hush," said a gentle voice. It was slow, a whisper. Annette tried to rise but the world tilted.

On the cusp of her vision stood two young men, and by them a collie that one of the lads was stroking.

"Donny and Rob. Eldest lads," explained Mary. "They found you."

"No time," Annette pleaded. "The man, he has my boy."

"There, there," Mary said gently. "Sit still a moment, Jack's gone for the police, they'll not be long. We know." Mary soothed as she gently eased Annette back into her chair.

"No, you don't understand," she winced. "He has my Duncan. He's so little. I need to go and find him."

"You're in no fit state to help anyone," a deep voice sounded. An older man came into vision. He stood beside his boys. "Let Mary tend to you. When the constables get here, we'll take the tractor. We'll take Laddie with us too. He'll trace your lad. Best tracker this one. Wiser than wandering the hills on your own."

Annette fought the panic rising within, wincing with each dab of Mary's cloth. But her vision began to clear. She saw the glass bowl in Mary's hand, the water clouded red. A living room. Rough farmhouse stone, photographs of prize bulls and family she could not quite make out. Horse brasses and rosettes above a fireplace; still glowing embers in a black iron hearth. A home. But one she couldn't stay in. Every second that was wasted meant her child could be further away from her and safety.

Annette nodded slightly. "How long? How long have I been here?"

"Not long."

And the falsehood hung in the air between them like a fine mist.

*

Police sergeant Martin Oliver folded his arms. At each shoulder stood officers Fennel and Murray. Whistles in pockets, truncheons at the waists, torches in hand. Their uniform buttons gleaming in the strange light afforded by the uncommon glow in the sky. A stubborn family of farmers stood before them in the yard.

"This is police business lads," Oliver said firmly. "There's protocol to be followed."

"My arse. People are dead, there's a bloody murderer on the loose and this poor woman was attacked in her own kitchen. Took her bairn. He's gone. Out there. And missing. What have you done about it!!!"

"You'll not go running around the hillside with shotguns. This is police business."

Mal snorted. "Business?" Feeding another cartridge into each barrel of his shotgun.

"We look after our own around here."

Sergeant Oliver's eyes darted to his two companions. "Jack!" Mary commanded. "Get the tractor and trailer."

Nodding, he started towards the sheds.

"You can't go out armed with shotguns," Oliver asserted.

"And what are you going to do to stop us?" Mal straightened, swinging his gun over his shoulder, Donny and Rob began hurriedly loading the trailer with weapons. Hammer, scythes, a wrench. Finally an old battered cricket bat.

"This is for Hen."

Annette darted towards the policemen. "Please! Let them go. You have not seen what I have, you must believe me! Look up there." She threw a hand towards the green-blue veil that hooded the hills.

"That's not natural is it? Is it?" She shouted now, a long, low strangled sound that pushed her away from the group and into the night, calling and calling the name of her child. If they answered, she never heard them for all sound in the world had disappeared.

As she ran towards the hills, Laddie at her heels, the farmers leapt onto the tractor. Behind them the three policemen scrambled for the car, racing across the field to the hill where the lightning spat upon the stones.

*

Dragging his eyes open, Duncan saw the dancing blue and green in the sky and remembered the sound that the lightning made as it hit the earth. He wanted his mummy. He was tired and so scared even though he knew he shouldn't be.

Something cold was beneath him, he tried to get up from the coldness but he couldn't. The old man hovered over him. "Foolish boy." Duncan tried to speak, but his tongue wouldn't listen.

"Foolish. You cannot move. Not yet. You took quite a bite." Dipping a thin paintbrush into a jar of red liquid he began to write on the stone upon which Duncan lay. He was very, very scared now, and he hurt inside, but not outside.

He couldn't move and couldn't call out. It was like a dream, but not one. If he closed his eyes again and thought of something lovely, like Mummy, or a pony, then maybe he would wake up back in his bed, with breakfast waiting for him downstairs and a trip to play with Bertie later.

But nothing happened. All he could do was lie there, still, wide-eyed with fear. The writing had stopped. Objects were being placed around him now. One above his head, at his feet, to his left and right. Duncan strained his eyes to look at the object to his left. It took the breath from his lungs. It was a heart. A heart. Just there. Next to him. He felt the warmth of it as the blood found rivulets in the stone and ran slowly towards him. That captured the colours dancing above them.

Beyond him, far away, the strange clock began to chime. He heard it from far away and yet very near, as the old man towered over him, jaw set in iron determination. Handfuls of white dust fell upon him from the small leather pouch that the Clockmaker held. All sense of hesitation or regret absent from his eyes.

He began to unbutton the boy's shirt. "Magic is as the first snows of winter. Powdering the ground, hinting of that to come. A reminder of blizzards from the past. Melting away and forgotten." The pot of red liquid replaced the leather pouch, as the old man began to brush fine symbols across his victim's chest.

"This, my Duncan, is a *kaptha*. A ritual bowl. Ah, that I had the minutes to tell you of its journey to you. For here, now in this world, we may see the lightest touches of magic. But mostly it melts away, driven away by the mechanisations of man. Such closed minds to old ways forgotten, lost in the earth."

Duncan felt the cold upon his chest and the wetness of the liquid as this man, once his friend, but now someone so frightening, continued his painting.

"Such a perfect canvas my dear. Such a perfect one." All Duncan could do was watch and listen in mute horror. "But then one day the snow comes back wild and fierce, cowering all those before it, as it blankets the earth. Tonight is one of those times Duncan. Tonight magic returns."

Raising his arms to the sky, he began to chant words, unknown to the child. Sounds that were beyond the human voice. Duncan felt the altar begin to shudder then vibrate with a slow, steady rhythm. He turned his head in horror as the heart next to him began to move, to beat. And then, Duncan began to scream.

Shrillings of fear and abject terror shook the air, startling the old man and silencing him. He glared at the boy.

"My, you are strong my Duncan," he said reaching for the castanet and beginning to click his tune. Duncan felt his pocket shift, the screams dying away within him and he turned his head. Looking down he saw his little pet begin to climb up his body.

"Buggy! Help me," the boy begged as the small construct slowly moved up to his breast to sit just above his heart. Colder than the paint that had now dried, the metal legs of his pet felt alien upon his body. A series of clicks and the tiny needles began to protrude from Buggy's head. Duncan whimpered.

Placing a hand on the boy's head, he lovingly smoothed his brow. "He is your friend Duncan; he will take the pain away. All the pain will go." Duncan's body spasmed as he felt the needles bite. Numbness crept into his bones, and he felt sleepy, so sleepy. With all his might he resisted, but his eyelids grew too heavy, far too heavy, as the little blue fairy fluttered above him. He thought he saw it smile until the sharp canines showed.

"Oh no," he whispered as he turned his head away from those who had betrayed his heart, that he had given so freely. He closed his eyes, barely seeing the pair of headlights lurching towards him.

XLVII

Snatch

The hairs on the back of Laddie's neck bristled as he began a low, snarled growling. He rose on his haunches, tensed and violent.

"That way," shouted Mal as Jack threw the tractor round in the direction of the dolmans. "Look at the light. There..." The trailer passengers rocked and swayed as Jack pushed the protesting engine to its limits.

In the distance they could see figures standing amidst the stones, a faint vast mist illuminating them. Where was the child? Someone called, but their voice whipped away as the swelling chant built and built till it echoed around them. Louder and louder it became until the noise was something you felt. A brick solid caterwaul of sound that drowned the engine's grinding and bent them down on their knees. Jack stamped on the brakes throwing the occupants forward as he clamped his hands over his ears.

"Mother of God!" he screamed. "Make it stop…"

"We'll handle this," shouted Oliver over the melee as the three officers jumped out of the police vehicle. Rob restrained Annette, holding her back. "Wait, just wait."

Screaming at him, she tried to break free from his grasp. "You don't understand," she said, over and over again as she struggled and the sound became a waterfall that drowned out all that they were.

*

The Clockmaker stood now above the prone body of the boy, holding an antique dagger as the blue smudge flitted around his shoulders. He looked at the knife in his hand. Ancient silver, blade curved, etched with fine filigreed designs from a forgotten age, a hidden souk between Arabic passageways he had frequented.

For a moment the melee swirling about this summit faded, and he felt once again the heat on his back as he moved between Phoenician shadows. Alleys that had no endings, but instead twined and writhed in an invisible maze, interrupted by doorways in which men stood, waiting. There had been no silks or saffron sellers in these openings, for he had no need for those.

His reasons for such visits had been myriad and

complex. A nod. A silent glance. And furtive transactions for poison and punishment. Such purchases had oftentimes been for masters, overlords. So many with their clamouring demands for power. Narcissists all.

But this. This beauty. This blade. This was it's time.

He recalled the man who had sold it to him. An antiquity of such rarity that few knew of its existence. Buried in the sands beyond Babylon.

Such beauty in this blade. Such a destiny that brought it to this moment. Here, where the only sound he wanted to hear was the final laboured breathing of the child and the beating of the four dead hearts on the *kudka* – the boundary stone between the then and the next.

*

What the shape was, Oliver was unable to tell, his eyes could not capture true form. The stones so stark against the swirl of the sky were not stones anymore, and these men were not men but noise that whipped him and beat him till he found he could not struggle past it. The two constructs stood like statues, arms raised like wings.

The old man chanted the obscene words, echoing again and again by the swaying ram and the goat. Vibrations deep in the ground poured up through the dolmans as the blue fairy darted around them. All was a blizzard of sound and form.

Battling towards the altar, Oliver raised his hand towards the old man.

"No need for this," he began. "Let the boy go, and let's

talk. Co-operate; no one will be harmed. Call those things off."

Warily, the old man eyed the approaching officers. "You know not what you meddle with. You would do well to leave me be."

"We can't do that. Stop all this, whatever it is, and put the knife down."

The Clockmaker glanced again at the officers and the men from the tractor. Annette, still restrained by a policeman.

"You brought the boy's mother?"

"Yes and some armed friends. Lower the knife before this gets out of hand."

He glanced at the knife in his hand. And placed it upon the chest of the child.

For a moment the only sound was the deep breathing of the unconscious boy and the beating of dead hearts.

Martin Oliver relaxed, taking a step forward. In a blur, the arm of the old man shot out and from his sleeve unfurled a snake of bone knots. The final image Oliver saw were the grasping fangs within a centipede's mouth before they buried themselves into the flesh of his face. As the creature wrapped its body around his neck, veins of black tar rippled across the skin of his cheeks. And he fell.

Raising his arms, the puppet master uttered one word, eclipsing the shrieking of storm and pain. "Kill!" Swiftly, the construct spun upon its axis, slicing the scythe of bladed bone into Murray's shoulder. Fennel rushed the leering ram with his truncheon.

273

Yelling curses, guns raised, the farmers raced up the slope. The horse turned its jittering attention towards them, jaw flapping as its screams joined the storm that raged upon the hill. Shotguns barked out as the construct buckled, shards of bone and cog flew, but still it came, dragging its leg behind it. Donny flew at the ram, smashing its head aside with the butt of his gun.

Annette ran towards her son, his name a constant scream, oblivious to the violence around her, or the pain that dragged inside her. Through the swarming creatures and the giants of black cloth. *To him.*

Mal was at her shoulder dragging her back by the arm. "Get off me," she screamed, pulling herself away, crawling across the broken ground as the sound pressed her further into the rough clod and rock. She felt her hands tear and knew she was breaking beneath the sound, but with everything she had left, she thrust herself towards the crest of the hill, oblivious to the violence around her. She crawled. Past Jack, buried beneath swarming metal insect constructs. Past the fallen horse construct. Past the ram flailing wildly with both Fennel and Donny clinging to its back.

She neither thought nor felt anything but rage now. Vengeance. Against the man whose chanting was roiling in her ears like a mockery, the blade held high above her son's chest. As she drew closer, the ram tossed its burden, and lumbered forward to intercept, crab claw striking and knocking her to the ground. It loomed above her, jaw chattering, raising its claw again, ready to strike. There was a shot. As the creature staggered it thrust the bone spike through Donny. Gasping in pain, he dropped the gun.

"One shot," he breathed through bloodied lips. "Just shoot him," looking for the last time at Annette, before the creature raised him above the ground and hurled him towards the grey stones.

Scooping up the gun Annette approached the altar. The Clockmaker had stopped chanting. Revulsion filled her as she took in the body of her prone child, the beating hearts arranged around him.

She hissed, "I.Will.Kill.You."

The Clockmaker looked at her with disdain in his eyes. "Here? You stupid weak, feeble woman," he roared. "Don't you see magic and power? Don't you?" His free hand spasmed, and from his sleeve he hurled a snarling rat construct towards her. She cowered, braced for the pain. Yet before its yawning jaws reached her, there was a piercing howl and the sound of bone shattering. Forcing her eyes open she saw Laddie shaking the creature; neck clamped tightly in his jaws. The chanting began again as the blue light darted around the old man.

Annette pointed the gun at the old man, his dagger raised to strike.

"You are the weak one," purred the blue fairy, in silken tones.

XLVIII

Peals

In here the footsteps echoed. They never rested. Not for a minute. The light was kept on in his cell and yet he heard no voices. He knew all too well what common criminals he nestled amongst. The thieves and fraudsters, black marketeers. Men who had returned to find their women had found other bed partners. And so took recourse in punishment.

And others. Equally dull. *For*. The world was two-dimensional to these men. The outside and the inside. Compartmentalised. Distinct. With roles and rules. Fleetingly, the Clockmaker wondered if that brought them comfort. But just as swiftly, dismissed the notion.

For.

The world he was still trapped within sliced through all concepts and history. A schism of parallels that for a brief moment splintered apart to reveal all his lives and the memories he hadn't recalled. All life was penance, it would appear.

Here, through a high window, he could see a monotony of grey clouds punctuating the days. The air in his cell had a bite to it that made him shiver beneath his blankets. This island's winters had never been kind. He had no idea where he was. He had travelled much since that night at the dolmans. Always shackled, always hooded. His trial had been brief.

At first they asked him to explain his actions. But they were common men, fools all. They saw merely the act of kidnapping. Nothing more. He remained as silent as he had in the bunker.

The military took an interest. Of course they would. What were the machines found near him on the hill? Had he known the makers of such? The assumption that he was too old and too frail to have made them. On and on. The questions and the ignorance. For hours. But those that questioned finally shook their heads and named him insane. Guilty. But insane.

He expected that on the morning of his execution he would feel restless panic. Yet he did not. His mind as calm and calculating as it had been the day he had fled the bunker. His body was still. He did not fear death. He knew that it was not the end. That his conscious mind would not cease with a snapping of his neck at the end of a noose. He knew that there was much behind the veil. The supernatural did exist. He had seen it; it was now as much a part of his story as his wonderful clocks and ingenious toys.

There would be a reckoning, there would be pain; perhaps not in a way the living understand it, but there would be pain. There was always pain and he was so very tarnished. But whatever reckoning there would be, he believed it would be fair. That was all that anyone could ever ask.

As each toll of the bell counted down the last minutes of his life, curious anticipation built up within him. He would cross the veil as a Columbus, a Raleigh or a Cook and discover new and distant lands.

There was still a second possibility. That death did not claim him this day. Would he fall through the gallows trapdoor, yet live on? What then? Would he defy death and rise again when the moment deemed?

These were not just the fantasies of a condemned man, nor hopes and dreams of one diagnosed with some incurable fatal disease. In truth he did not know the answer.

When the demons came and reminded him of his sins as he slept, he felt them squirm and mock. Did he still have his power? Yes, he had been shot on that hill that night. But it was a shotgun blast from a distance too far away to be lethal. It had hurt him, of course.

As he lay on his back by the altar, blood from his wound pooling around him, he saw the dybbuk vanish. With it, all the fight he had left went with it. They beat him, dragging him away, baying their victory. But he had healed.

As always.

He did not fully understand what had happened on that fateful night up amongst the standing stones. The dybbuck had the power to grant him what he wished for, but had it betrayed him and chosen the younger vessel on which to work its magic?

Had that always been its intention? Had he just been a pawn in a game? Had it known all that time what it wanted, who it wanted? *Duncan?* Had it lain in the depths of the bunker, waiting, waiting for him, knowing all along he would come and claim it as his own? That it would use the book to guide him along the path it had designed for him to follow. All those miles he had travelled, all the innocent blood he had shed, the lives he had ruined. It was not how his story was meant to end.

Perhaps the reckoning that awaited him was, in fact, the mortal side of the veil. And that if today death did not find him, tomorrow he would seek out the dybbuck. As possibilities began to wind their way through his mind, the last knoll of the bell sounded, the last grain of hourglass sand fell, and at the door stood the Clockmaker's last priest.

The schism jittered and he saw.

XLIX

Schism

A loud thud on the ceiling above told Annette that Duncan was finally out of bed. She had busied herself in the kitchen that morning. Though many weeks had passed since that night in the hills, her sleep was fitful and sporadic. Yet Duncan would sleep for hour upon hour. But she knew his slumber was not peaceful either. She would hear him cry out as the night terrors came. Calling her name, for his father, even the old man on the odd occasion.

She would slip into his room, then gently climb into his bed and cradle him in her arms till his cries became whimpers that stilled into sleep as she stroked him.

That monstrous man and his creatures; how he had wormed his way into their home, her family, the heart of her boy. Often the anger came unannounced and she would walk the lakeside for hours in an attempt to find tranquillity. They say time heals, but some things leave an echo that can never be truly silenced. An echo she feared she would hear always, no matter how faint it became.

Doctors assured her that Duncan was strong, resilient. It would take time but he would recover. Youth, they had said, is a remarkable age. The war children, evacuees, had shown them that, they announced. They... an army of doctors, experts, policemen and priests, even military men, who had spent endless hours of interviews with her and Duncan. Curiosity at the root of their questions. But they were not the ones who heard his night cries nor comforted him in the dark.

It was not them who gave her and her son comfort or reassurance. That was found in the terraced house in Chillingham Road in Newcastle. One day she packed their bags and ran. Boarded a train and headed south of the border to Walter and Nora and little Anne.

They listened, never doubted, never questioned. With Nora's wise counsel and Walter's humour – jokes and pranks – Duncan began laughing again. She refound her happy, inquisitive child who now insisted on getting a puppy. A collie, whom he decided they would name "Laddie the little".

In the evening, while the children slept, she would talk to them by firelight.

"To kill a monster you must first look it in the eye,"

Walter had told her. "During the war, in Africa, in the desert, we saw some strange things, things we couldn't believe…"

"You have to go back, pet. You have to front it out," Nora would say. "Give it a week or so, see how it feels. And if it doesn't sit well, come back; there is always a place here for you and your lad."

It was terrifying, the thought of returning. But she knew they were right. Knew that if she waited longer then the fear would always second-guess her and win.

They boarded the northbound train the following week, waved off by the Fosters and laden with food for the journey and the first evening in their old home. She tried very hard not to cry for Duncan's sake, tried hard to summon the bravery she had found that night when the sky split with colour and anger. Tried hard not to doubt her decision.

This journey was not one of Spitfires nor sweets. There were no men on the train who offered her child chocolate. It was a journey of stoppings and startings, of muffled conversations between strangers she had no wish to meet. Of landscapes that became barren the further they travelled.

Dolly had been into the house during their absence; cleaning the bloodstains off the kitchen floor, changing linen and pushing wide the windows. There had been fresh bread on the table when they arrived, some supplies neatly stacked in the larder and flowers from a garden in the village. And a note from Bertie to Duncan. Would he like to come and play? Yes, nodded Duncan, he would.

It took some days before Annette could muster the courage to go into the village. Between the memory of the night and her behaviour, there hung a deep embarrassment that she had shown herself to be weak. Shrieking and wailing in front of strangers was something she would never have suspected she would do. Dolly assured her that the townsfolk felt only sympathy and care towards her. But still…

As they took a turn around the village, people nodded, some passed them by with sympathetic smiles, some came merely to gossip, others to congratulate and tell them how brave they were facing the mad man and his monsters. Some even called her a hero. And that made her blush.

Duncan's classmates visited him, determined to be friends with "Duncan the monster hunter". But despite these lovely moments of returning, the shroud of the Clockmaker still clung to the area. Local newspapers spoke of clicking objects moving in the long grass, of robed giants lurching through the hill fog, with crab claws for hands and a ram skull for a head. But no photographs were ever produced to go along with such stories.

And gradually, gradually, things settled and faded and the autumn colours swept in, and it was time for night fires and hot chocolate with a book at bedtime. The house was becoming more of a home now. She had taken many of the pictures from the attic rooms, and rehung them in the downstairs rooms. Images of past lives and histories. It was fitting she thought, that they should be a part of the change in the house.

Dolly had found her a handy man, a lad called Iain, who had painted some of the walls, varnished the wood and hung paper in the kitchen. It was astonishing the difference it made.

The objects that Duncan had found in the outhouse had been retrieved, polished and replaced in the sideboard dresser. Some were so lovely she had displayed them on the surface.

One thing she had made a point of doing, with the help of Dolly and Iain, was to remove the taxidermy heads from the walls. They reminded both her and her child of the night-monsters high up on that fateful hill. Iain had burnt them.

They had had a couple of guests since their return. Duncan had been wary at first, and that was to be expected. The couple, a Dr and Mrs Cameron from Edinburgh had assured her that they would recommend her hotel to others. Perhaps she could get some postcards made of Loch House and its surroundings? They would have liked to have sent several to friends and family. That was a very good idea, Annette had said.

*

Duncan came into the kitchen, still in his new pajamas that Nora had made for him. They were red tartan because he was a Highland lad now, she had said. He wasn't smiling this morning and she thought perhaps he was ill. Or tired. She asked him if he had slept well and got no response.

Sitting down at the kitchen table he picked at the shell of the egg, pushing the buttered toast around the edge.

"It's today, isn't it Mummy?"

Ah. That was it. Annette nodded. "Yes Duncan, it is."

"Will it hurt him, do you know?"

"I don't know, my love. I believe it is very quick." Annette cracked the eggshell for him and cut up the toast into strips. "Are you hungry?" she asked and he shook his head.

"I thought I was because my tummy said so, but now I think it is sadness."

She didn't know what to say. After everything they had been through, her fragile and gentle child still clung to the time when the man had been his friend. A friend who had taken him fishing and played pooh sticks. Who knew so much and would listen.

Silently the tears came and he bowed his head. Reaching for him, she knelt down and held him as his shoulders trembled and she wondered when he had become so thin. Why hadn't she seen this change? Tomorrow she would take him to the new doctor in the village. And get him some tonic, and build him back up.

"Duncan," she soothed, "what he did was very, very bad my love." He nodded and said yes, he knew.

"Then don't be sad my darling. There are lovely things to look forward to here. Bertie is coming and we can all go out on the lake. Would you like that?"

"I'm not sad for him, Mummy. It's just that I don't like it here anymore."

"Is it the bad dreams?"

He shook his head. "I don't have bad dreams anymore, not really… Mummy, it's because one monster stayed."

"Oh Duncan, there are no more monsters." Looking him in the eye she said, "The policemen caught them all. You know that, don't you?"

Pleading eyes looked up at her. "They didn't catch all of them Mummy, they missed one."

"No they didn't." she sighed. "They caught them all; I was there. Remember?"

Duncan nodded. "Yes. But Mummy… one followed us home; it's upstairs, behind my glass. It has been there all along."

A sliver of fear threaded her spine, leaving a gnawing doubt with its passing. Could there be? Could there be one more… could he have left one here to trap them long after he had gone? Could one of his blasphemous creations have found its way back to its lair?

Yet neither of them had been attacked. There had been no strangeness here since their return. Their days had passed calmly. Friends and outings and kindness. The guests.

She sighed. The doctors had said he would recover but there were bound to be times when he remembered the details.

"Let's go and get rid of it shall we?" she smiled. Duncan hesitated, but let her take his hand.

She entered his bedroom first. Duncan paused in the doorway and then followed her in. He picked up his dressing gown. Through the window, grey pre-winter clouds hung low in the sky, obscuring the waking sun.

That's all there is in the glass, she said to him, just our lovely outside world. Soon it would be colder, she thought. And reminded herself to check the coal in the outhouse.

Bending down she peered under his bed. "Nothing here. Where shall I check next? Up the chimney? In your slippers? How about behind your ears?" Expecting laughter, she turned to smile at him.

He held something in his hands, which he thrust towards her, an odd expression on his face. It was a thick book.

"What is this my love…" she asked. "Did you get this from the attics? What is it about? I found a lovely one up there a while ago. Fairy tales and legends."

"It's his. He wants you to have it."

It was made of dark brown thin leather. There was no title or picture. No words on the spine. How odd. She opened it; nothing but empty curled yellowing pages. Her fingertips brushed over the ridged surface, ribbed and wrinkled.

"Duncan?" The appearance of the book began to nibble at the edges of her calm. "Where did you get this?"

"He's not under the bed or in the cupboards. Not in that glass in the window, he's in this one here."

Following the boy's gaze towards the mirror set into the wardrobe door, the book slipped from her fingers. There in the glass, standing in a brown dressing gown, half thrown over tartan pajamas, a pair of feline amber eyes, flecked with cobalt, smiled beneath a mop of red hair. Skin an unclean marble, cracked with veins of pitch split into a smile of tiny pointed teeth roped with viscous oily saliva.

"Hello Mummy."

287

ACKNOWLEDGMENTS

We both wish to thank the following people, whose patience, encouragement and suggestions have led to this book's completion.

To Ana Priscila Rodriquez Aranda for her beyond beautiful artwork.

Netta Boundy for her experience, constructive criticism and love through this.

To Alison Harding, for being an editor, critic and third wheel.

Lisa Mc Donald and Collette Murphy for their insight from the off.

And to John Salisbury and Ash Brookes of Weekend warlords, Loughborough: The Leicester All Scars and all at Tabletop Tyrant Leicester.

And to all our wonderful friends and family, who supported us, proofread and held our hands throughout the writing of this book. It is from their encougement we are writing more.

Thank you one and all, we love you.

Ceri and Drew x

THE PERFECT CHILD

November 2nd.

Tis All Souls day my dear.

Ah. Yes, so I believe. And most cold and violent this weather dear sir.

It is dark in the passageways and tunnels where bricks weep with the rain and the snow that refuses to melt. So dark that the colours run and the browns become the yellows and the ochres of your skirts.

And my shawl is too thin in the wind.

Fog makes it worse though would you not agree? Listening for the footfalls and coughs. Voices in the ale houses and hoarse breathings upon bare necks. Fog from the stacks and the factories. Fog from the coal fires in terraced houses or those that fall behind the twitchels and alleys.

A mistress she is, that strides through the city turning

day into a twilight and forlorn relic. A phlegmlike collicky mass that catches your throat and makes the young ones thinned by laudanum waste away upon soiled matresses of poverty.

But my shawl is too thin for this wind.

Can you hear the sound though. Below this weathery day. A stillness that echoes?

I feel it sir. Some 200 miles and a century away... Something twisted weaving patterned slippers upon these cobbles. Velvet feet.

Waiting for him by the gate near a darkened yard, the mist in the passages swirled about like a black overcoat. Oh she gasped. For handsome he was. He was. Not in that wholesome way that farm folk have, nor the coarse hoarseness of bar men and sailors who docked in her tunny thrice weekly.

Change? Will you pin me to the wall or hoik my skirts and say *how much*?

And is your shawl still too thin for this loving?

Hush hush...

She would be the first of the 5 to feed its soul. She had heard the sound deep within her.She cocked her head to listen to it but shrugged and said I can't.

Dark and bearded. What do you smell like?

Was that the sound of horse hooves? Did she see a blackened carriage pound away down Denman Street?

A bit.

He hands her grapes. Hungry? A bit. How kind? Thank you sir. For these are a rarity for one such as she. Wrapped loosely in a red kerchief. Sits warmly in her palm. Yes.

Lowered them into her mouth. Her reflection in the iris of his eye. It was dark and stroked her. Deep down. Now.

Where had he come from? The roof tops? Had he been a loving?

Sneaking between sheets with some wife who did the deed? Did they rustle under you? No matter. Give me money for a rough house. For the ruin of mothers. For a night in a bed with 5 others?

As he stepped to her and lifted her underskirt. *I no longer care.*

The final words I will ever hear are

"You will want to say anything but your prayers..."

OPTICS

The gentle vibration of the walls of his room heralded the approach of incoming craft. Tutting, Mourd-Vatura dragged his gaze from the screen he had been staring at for the last half an hour, and made a mental note to upgrade the dampening technology cocooning his office rooms.

He stood up from his chair, smoothed down the jet fabric of his suit and quickly crossed the brief distance to the sole window in the room. A hemispherical bubble of armoured glass that was taller than he was. He lamented the loss of the aperture's previous covering- a rich mosaic of panes said to have been recovered from some of Earth's last churches.

When the sun was high they had cast clouds of colour on the lush white carpet. As the sun journeyed across the horizon, the colours would drift with it, a slow waltz around one another in an afternoon's dream. That window had indeed been a work of art. The glass long lost now, scattered to the four winds, the window destroyed beyond repair when he had thrown the room's previous occupant through it.

As the gentle vibration grew into a low- key hum, Mourd pursed his lips. His pale face was sharp cut, elongated, predatory. A narrow long nose twitched below eyes of total pitch, shark like. Framed in heavy lidded slits that conveyed callous calculation. His raven hair, thinning slightly now, close cut and waxed in to rows of stout, sharp cones. He took a deep breath and bounced once on shined patent leathered toes. He clasped his hands behind his back and waited. The view was just as he liked it. The atmospheric cleansers had done an admirable job.

The sky was now an open blue. Below him, as far as the eye could see, swirled the clouds, broken only by the thrusting spire in which he stood. A fitting view for his exalted role within the Great Machine.

His wait was not a long one. The air whistled to the tune of jet engine noise as a great golden hooked beak came into view. Vast eyes shone from an eagle's head, a fuselage of sculpted golden feathers stretched back behind it. The workmanship was that of a supreme artisan.

Whatever weaponry the craft carried was hidden inside wide swept back wings of gilded plumage. A thin smile ticked at the corners of his mouth. Flying this close to the spires was an offence. The pilot was either brave or foolish but possibly useful. Perhaps the craft would be the only thing he took from him.

For now.

*

Distraction over, he returned to his desk and the business of the hour on the three large monitor screens. To his left the smaller screen for personal communication. To his right, a much larger rectangle of winking stars charting the known universe. And before him sat a tall square that was the current focus of his attention. Camera feeds from the tunnels that led into the belly of the Great Machine. Below each monitor was housed the mass of electronics that facilitated his link deep into the central intelligence hub of the Great Machine.

Its screen was tiled with grainy images. Each showing processions of hunched humanity drudging through the tunnels towards a daily toil on the production lines.

Watching the human cattle on their way to a new shift was beneath one of such a lofty position as he. But something had begun to irk him. Power outages - just for a few brief seconds- at the same time every day, at the beginning of the same shift. The flow of energy had never paused inside the workings of the Great Machine before, and this now bothered him.

Investigations had found no probable cause, simply that the problem originated within the tunnels. A simply anomaly that would smooth itself out the overseers reports had told him. He did not like anomalies. He did not believe in them. His eyes scanned through the images, trudging masses, nothing unusual until a red light flashed on the adjoining screen.

He spun on his chair and looked at the screen displaying

the star map. The light informed him something had changed in the void, something was moving. The distance interstellar communications had to travel were impossibly vast; it would take a moment for the screen to display the new information.

As he waited impatiently, his dark gaze lingered on one of his most coveted possessions. Ah that he had been alive to witness such an historic event. It portrayed a titan, a goat headed creature that stood ankle deep in the mire, dangling a man from its fingers on puppet strings above a burning fire. The hem of the man's bloody robes singe and wisps of grey, like ash smeared on glass, begin to float in the air; the souls of reluctant dead.

Over many years the Earth's populace had been nudged into sin and cruelty, fuelling the Lord of the Underworld. As the power of God waned, the Arch Angel gorged himself upon the sin of mankind until satiated he rose from the pit to slay God his creator.

The star chart display revealed the image .A whirlpool of colour before it settled. A blood stain that pooled outward from humanity's birth world, crimson waters oozing across the firmament. The spread of the Arch Angel himself and his entourage, pillaging the colonised worlds, moving on from one to another until he grew tired of toying with their populations and began his advance to the deeper reaches. Yet still many life times away from world of the Great Machine.

With a shrug he turned his attention to the shuffling hordes. All the images were of the same fooled labouring masses toiling their lives away within the Great Machine; with the constructed fiction that their work would one day resurrect God.

Yet on one small screen tile, one image was different. The time scrolling in the bottom corner had frozen. He ignored the others and brought this one to full screen. It was not of a tunnel but a wider space. An intersection. The mass of grey hunched figures were funneling into the forge. All bar two.

The image jerked with static then returned. Two figures had stopped. One thick set and tall, hooded, his back to the camera, unmoving. The other smaller, also hooded, and although smeared with dirt was clearly female. Beneath the hood he saw a curl of colour. A twist of sunshine amongst all that grey. A lock of hair.

Workers had their hair cropped, to prevent parasites. This one had disobeyed and hidden it from the overseers. The cattle could not disobey! Static snowed the screen again. Mourd stared at the screen. The female stared back at him. She was looking directly into the camera; how could she even know of its existence, camouflaged as they all were.

She could see it. His heavy fist hit the desk. The image snowed again, static danced, longer this time, anger and frustration began to boil within him. What he next saw made him rise to his feet and curse. The masses were gone. Long since departed to their work stations. Only two remained. The female and the male at her shoulder stared back. The static returned and when the screen cleared, the intersection was empty.

He opened communications to the secretary. " Bring Executive Zeetees and find me Eradicator Barrett," he hissed. "I have work for them to do."